ONE COWARDLY AMBUSH . . .

Longarm stepped up on the plank walk to see that there really was a LeMat nine-shooter for sale in the front window.

Someone had written in High Dutch and English on a card propped against the trigger guard of the dramatic weapon. Longarm bent lower to read what the English writing said. That was why the bullet aimed at the nape of his neck just took his hat off for him as it flew on to shatter that plate glass all to flying bits!

Longarm
and the Kansas Killer

**THE SPECIAL 200th JUBILEE EDITION
OF TODAY'S MOST POPULAR
ADULT WESTERN!**

→ TABOR EVANS ←

LONGARM

AND THE
KANSAS KILLER

JOVE BOOKS, NEW YORK

LONGARM AND THE KANSAS KILLER

A Jove Book / published by arrangement with
the author

PRINTING HISTORY
Jove edition / August 1995

ISBN: 0-515-11681-5

A JOVE BOOK®
Jove Books are published by The Berkley Publishing Group,
200 Madison Avenue, New York, New York 10016.
JOVE and the "J" design are trademarks
belonging to Jove Publications, Inc.

PRINTED IN THE UNITED STATES OF AMERICA

10 9 8 7 6 5 4 3 2 1

Chapter 1

No sober soul with a lick of common sense would have breezed through the entrance of the wildest whorehouse in Denver without a certain wariness. So the gun-muzzle gray eyes of the tall lawman in a tobacco tweed suit stared thoughtfully from under the brim of his dark telescoped Stetson, and the tail of his coat hung clear of the .44-40 riding cross-draw on his left hip as he wondered why things seemed so quiet on a Saturday night in the greenup time in cattle country.

There were no customers at all in the downstairs taproom as he entered it. The soiled doves who'd usually be prancing and dancing moped all about with long faces. Some of them were crying. When a frightened-looking young colored gal in a French maid's outfit timidly approached to tell him they'd just closed for the night, their tall tanned visitor explained, laconically but not unkindly, "I ain't here for fun. I'd be Deputy U.S. Marshal Custis Long. I've been told your madam, Emma Gould, was after me for some service she's unable to provide."

The whorehouse maid tried to take his hat, and when that didn't work, she scampered out of the taproom as one whore murmured to the one seated next to her, "That's him, the one they call Longarm! Ain't he good-looking, though?"

1

Before the object of this professional appraisal could feel all that silly, the madam herself was waving him into the back with a pint or so of diamonds wrapped around a plump wrist. So he went to join her, looking neither to his right nor left as half-clad gals who should have been ashamed of themselves made rude observations about what they could see of him and crude speculations as to what a strange gent might have concealed under his own private duds.

The madam told him to pay the sassy things no mind, and hauled him into her businesslike office to sit him down as she hauled out a bottle of Maryland Rye. Then she asked if he recalled the time he'd said he owed her.

Longarm smiled up at the once pleasantly plump and now just fat old pal. "I sure do, Madame Emma. For it was not long ago on the slopes of Capitol Hill that you saved my bacon. I was just across Colfax Avenue without a care in the world when your dulcet scream rent the air and that backshooter you'd spotted shot an old shade tree instead."

"I just wanted you to say you still owed me," the most prosperous madam in Denver told him. "One of my girls is laying on a cold zinc table in the county morgue, and who's going to take a colored kid's word against those of two mining magnates, backing one another up, the murderous high-toned bastards!"

Longarm held up a weary hand and pleaded, "Rein in, back up, and start at the beginning."

So Emma Gould began. "It commenced about eleven this evening. A couple of mining magnates called Carbonate Ned Cartier and Telluride Tommy Gordon blew in, well oiled, after the management had asked them to leave a fussier establishment. They drank some more out front, and then they naturally went upstairs with a couple of my girls to enjoy some unnatural acts. Neither was sober enough to enjoy a woman the old-fashioned way."

Longarm reached for a smoke, but held the three-for-a-nickel cheroot aloft for her silent permission or denial. "I was

2

wrong. I didn't want you to start *too* far back. Get to how one of your gals wound up in the morgue.''

Emma Gould nodded at the cheap but not too pungent cheroot. ''I'm getting to that, dammit. As I said, the only witness was our colored maid, Willow. Frenching Ann and the aging but tidy Telluride Tommy seemed to be getting along all right in *her* crib. Willow says most of the ugly talk was coming from Baltimore Barbara's crib as she was trying in vain to pleasure that unpleasant Carbonate Ned. Willow can't say what the trouble in there might have been. I promised her family when they let her come to work for me that I'd never use their virgin child for such services. How was I to know she'd fill out so tempting? But I'd given my word, and Willow doesn't know enough about such things to say just what might have gone wrong. She can say, however, she was standing right there in the doorway with the drinks the brute had ordered when he simply rolled off poor Baltimore Barbara and threw her headfirst out a side window as if she'd been a rag doll some vicious child was tired of playing with!''

Longarm finished lighting his cheroot before he grimaced and remarked, ''We are talking about a second-story window over an alley, right?''

The madam nodded grimly and explained, ''She landed on her head and broke her neck. She looked so innocent—all right, peaceful—lying there with her eyes half open and a dreamy smile on her painted lips. We naturally called the Denver P.D. Lord knows they make us pay the machine enough. So our neighborhood roundsmen took both of the surly drunks in. Sergeant Nolan, on the desk tonight, says they're good for at least the rest of the night in jail.''

Longarm nodded thoughtfully at the glowing tip of the cheroot in one hand and declared, ''I know Sergeant Nolan. He's a good man. He'll show them both as hard a time as they deserve. Or as hard a time as he can manage leastways.''

The irate Emma Gould scowled and said, ''Nolan suggested I get in touch with you when I allowed I knew you as well.

3

He seems to think *you're* good too, Custis.''

Longarm protested, ''Hold on! I ride for Marshal Vail and a *federal* district court, Madame Emma. I don't have jurisdiction over a local whorehouse killing, no offense. If I did, I fail to see what I could do any better than your local copper badges. They arrested the both of them when only one threw that gal out the window, right?''

Emma Gould sighed and softly replied, ''I wish you wouldn't try to bullshit an old whore who's been lied to by slick-talking men all her misspent life! Carbonate Ned is backing Gordon's tale that neither one of them had anything to do with the demise of some drunken doxie. They're willing to swear in court that they'd both enjoyed the dubious charms of two other drunks and were fixing to leave when, for whatever reason of her own, Baltimore Barbara just decided she was a real dove with the wings to fly her up to the statehouse and once around the dome. When Sergeant Nolan asked Cartier why he didn't try to stop her, the sarcastic bastard just laughed and said they were all so drunk he'd thought she might make it.''

Longarm snorted smoke out both nostrils and asked what the other white gal recalled of the ugly scene.

Emma Gould shrugged and replied, ''Not a thing. Frenching Ann has to get good and drunk before she'll go down on a man without crying. She says it makes her feel homesick.''

Longarm thought and murmured, ''In sum, it's the word of your young lady of color against that of two upstanding pillars of the boys-will-be-boys community.''

It had been a statment rather than a question. The unhappy Emma Gould still replied, ''Exactly. Sergeant Nolan says as soon as he has to let them send for their high-priced and well-connected lawyers come morning, they'll surely walk out the front door on writs, and if the case ever comes to trial their lawyers will make browned hash out of poor Willow. She's a smart little thing, and as honest as anyone working in a whorehouse could be expected to be, but just the same, the only witness for the prosecution, should anyone in the district attorney's office feel that silly, would still strike the jury as a colored girl who works in a whorehouse!"

Longarm rose to his considerable height as he sighed and told the visibly pessimistic old bawd, "You and Nolan are both right. Before we go down to the county jail we'd best pick up another old pal from that flea circus and museum of natural wonders on Larimer Street. *He* owes *me*. So I'm sure he'll be proud to gather up some tools of his trade and tag along to the morgue with us."

Emma Gould reached for a shawl to wrap around her plump bare shoulders as she looked bewildered. "We're taking a sideshow man to the county morgue with us? Whatever for, Custis? They say there's no mystery about poor Baltimore Barbara's death. Cartier threw her out the window and she broke her neck. Willow saw it happen!"

Longarm nodded and said, "We're all agreed on what happened. But we need more witnesses to prove it. So we'd best go scout some up!"

Chapter 2

Spending the night in jail gets to be less fun after midnight. So by three A.M. the older, less guilty, and scared-sober Telluride Tommy Gordon was pacing the cement floor at the far end of the cell block. The younger but more grizzled Carbonate Ned Cartier reclined on a hardwood bunk as if he thought he'd been asked to pose for a painting of Queen Cleopatra. Both prisoners, as befitted their newfound fortunes, were dressed in rumpled but still mighty expensive duds, although their diamond studs and such now resided for safekeeping up front.

From the bunk the beetle-browed Cartier growled, "Will you for Pete's sake simmer down, old son? If I've told you once I've told you a hundred times that I'll buy you a swell breakfast at that all-night restaurant at Union Station. There's just no way you can hold a man with a good lawyer during business hours, and by this time or way earlier tomorrow, we'll look back on all this shit and laugh."

His more worried companion replied, "The hell you say! You killed that gal dead as a turd in a milk bucket, and I've heard tell old Madame Emma has her *own* fancy lawyers on retainer!"

The bearish mine owner who'd thrown Baltimore Barbara

out that window naked as a jay shrugged a massive shoulder. "Was old Emma Gould up yonder with us? The only one in this world who saw me teaching that whore to fly was another whore, and a nigger besides. I'd have never told you what I'd just done if you hadn't come tearing in before I'd had time to gather my wits. I told you true when I told you I'd been aiming her at the wall across the room, the more fool I. But by that time the nigger wench had run off screaming, and she never heard us working out a more gentle way to explain that dumb cunt's suicide."

"I must have been out of my mind as well as drunk!" moaned Gordon. "I never had to get my ass in this sling to begin with! I could have just said I was messing with another drunk next door and didn't know nothing. But no, I had to lie like a rug to the police when they showed up, and now I'm in the same fool boat with you!"

"See that your remember that!" Cartier warned as a disturbance down at the far end of the long corridor caught Gordon's attention.

Most of the usual Saturday night crowd had been bailed out by now. But there were still enough drunks closer to the front to supply some catcalls and whistles as what seemed like a cluster of six or eight newcomers moved slowly along the dimly lit corridor.

By this time Cartier had noticed the changes in the air as well, and rolled off the hard bunk to join Gordon at the bars across the front of their cell. He was the one who suggested that maybe someone had gotten to at least one of their lawyers.

Gordon wasn't as rosy as he peered through the gloom to make out one taller cuss with his Stetson crushed North Range style, a trio of somewhat shorter men in blue uniforms, and what seemed to be at least three women. It was tough to be certain. One of the skirted figures seemed to be having trouble walking. So the others with her had to bunch close to help her along.

As if impatient, the tall man in the Stetson and low-heeled

army boots, separated by a three-piece suit, forged forward with a more familiar, shorter, and huskier-looking Sergeant Nolan of the Denver P.D.

As the two of them passed a coal oil wall lamp Gordon moaned, "Oh, Jesus, it's that deputy marshal they keep writing about in the *Rocky Mountain News*! They call him Longarm and they say he's good!"

Cartier snorted, "It can't be him. He's a federal man and killing whores ain't no federal offense."

As the two lawmen drew even nearer, the beetle-browed killer took a deep breath, let half of it out so his voice wouldn't crack, and softly added, "Even if it's him, just remember they haven't got anything on us as long as we stick together, pard!"

"What's this *us* shit?" Gordon muttered in a barely audible voice.

But as Longarm and Nolan bellied up to the far side of the bars and Nolan asked if anyone would like to change their story, Gordon shook his head just as hard as his guilty pal did.

Longarm smiled wolfishly through the bars. "It sure warms my heart to get two for the price of one," he said. "I've yet to see a rich man hang. So what the hell. It sounds almost as good to nail both you chumps on attempted murder as just one of you for manslaghter or, in this case, galslaughter."

Cartier snorted, "Dream on, cowboy! We're both saying she jumped! It's our word against a nigger whore who tried to shake us down for more than her backing was worth, see?"

Longarm just laughed sort of dirty. Sergeant Nolan half turned to call back down the corridor, "Why don't you boys just pick the poor gal up and carry her?"

Emma Gould shouted back, "They tried. She says it hurts. I swear I don't see why you couldn't leave her in County General where such a dreadfully injured girl belongs!"

As the madam shouted her reply, the bunch with her was passing a wall fixture. So there was no mistaking the pale but gamely smiling face of that one gal on crutches as Madame Emma and Willow, the colored maid, braced her from either

9

side with copper badges front and rear.

Telluride Tommy Gordon sobbed, "Jesus H. Christ! You told me you'd *killed* her, you loco bastard!"

Cartier snapped, "Shut up! It's some trick!"

But his older and smaller cellmate whined on. "They're right about both of us going to state prison if they can prove we've been fibbing, and *I* never laid a *hand* on the bitch!"

He didn't get to say more than that as Cartier threw a round-house that sat him in a far corner with a fat bloody lip. Nolan shoved a key in the lock with a curse. "You hit that poor old man again and the two of us are going to have it out, me darling bully boy!"

Cartier stayed put, gripping a bar with each fist as he glared through the bars at the approaching procession. "I aimed you at the durned *wall*, Baltimore Barbara!" he snarled. "You tell 'em I was only out to jar some sense into you when you took it into your own head to dive out the durned window instead!"

The pallid gal on crutches stopped a few yards off in the gloom, as if to gather strength for a final charge, as meanwhile Longarm jeered, "I'm sure both the judge and the jury will buy a gal you can screw for a dollar diving headfirst out a second-story window as an added thrill. What did she do to get you so riled, laugh at the size of your dick?"

Carbonate Ned Cartier drew himself grandly erect to protest, "Ain't nothing wrong with this child's dick! Ask Baltimore Barbara yonder if it wasn't herself who said I was hung too heroic for her to take me Greek style!"

Nolan quietly asked, "Is that why you got sore at her?"

Cartier shrugged and sheepishly replied, "Wouldn't you? I'd paid the house three dollars for three ways and she'd only taken me two. When I told her it was hardly fair to charge a man for three ways, then only take him two, she laughed and said there was nothing in any contract calling for either party to accomplish the impossible."

Longarm noticed the older man in the corner seemed to be trying to get back up while drooling blood. He saw Nolan had

10

noticed the same and finished unlocking the cell door. So all Longarm said was, "Let's see if we can get this straight. Was it her refusal to do it or her laughing about it that inspired you to toss her out the window?"

Cartier was too smart to answer. But the battered Telluride Tommy blubbered from his far corner, "He said it was the names she called him from the Good Book!"

Cartier snapped, "Shut up, you stupid old fart!"

But the erstwhile pal he'd injured snapped back, "I'll show you who's stupid! She was citing Genesis Nineteen, in which the Lord God rains down fire and brimstone on the men of Sodom for trying to corn-hole some angels he'd sent to visit with Abraham and his nephew Lot. Don't you remember telling me the only thing that riled you more than a cheating whore was a bible-thumping whore, Ned?"

Cartier told him to do a dreadful thing to his poor old mother.

Longarm asked Nolan, "You reckon that'll do it?"

The burly sergeant called back, "Have you got it all on paper for the D.A., Wojensky?"

The police stenographer waved his shorthand pad under a nearby wall lamp and cheerfully called back, "Every word, Sarge."

So Nolan turned back to the men inside the bars. "We won't bother you gents any more for now, unless either one of you has more to say."

Telluride Tommy shouted, "Let me out of here and get me away from this mad dog and I'll have *plenty* to say! I was only trying to back a pal to begin with, and you just saw how he treats everybody he can *git* at, the crazy-mean son of a bitch!"

So Nolan hauled him out into the corridor before Cartier could hit him again, then slammed and locked the door again and suggested the remaining prisoner try to get some rest, seeing he'd be facing a long day come sunrise.

As Nolan and Longarm walked the bloody but unbowed

11

older man back to the others, Telluride Tommy nodded to the wan-looking figure on crutches and said softly, "You know I had nothing to do with hurting you, and I'm glad you didn't die after all, Miss Barbara."

Then he took a second look, stepped closer, and exclaimed, "What in blue blazes?"

So Longarm told him, not unkindly, "That bad-tempered pal you just parted company with was right to begin with. It was all a trick."

Chapter 3

Everyone needed at least a little sleep. So it was a tad late the next morning when Longarm strode innocently into the office of Marshal William Vail of the Denver District court and was told with a knowing smile by young Henry, the squirt who played the typewriter out front, that this time he was really going to get it.

Longarm shrugged, lit his own cheroot in self-defense, and went on back to the oak-paneled inner office of their boss, the stubby and crusty old Billy Vail. Longarm had skimmed the morning edition of the *Denver Post* while having ham, eggs, and chili con carne with black coffee and mince pie for breakfast. His occasional drinking companion and occasional nemesis, Reporter Crawford, hadn't made up any lies about him this time, and whorehouse killings were only reported, if at all, on page three. So what the hell.

As he entered the marshal's private chambers with his own smoke gripped at a jaunty angle between his grinning teeth, Longarm saw at a glance that the older lawman seated behind a cluttered desk had him beat by miles as a human volcano. The blue haze Longarm had to wade through to the leather guest chair on his side of the desk didn't hurt his eyes half as much as the smell afflicted his nose. He knew for a fact that his boss paid more for those gnarly black cigars, and old Billy didn't seem to think it was funny when you asked if he was smoking mummified bats or simply bat shit.

Taking a seat and blowing a bubble of sweeter smoke by far, Longarm nodded at the banjo clock on an oak-paneled wall, allowed he was sorry about arriving later than usual, and asked how soon he could go to lunch.

Vail scowled through the haze and growled, "Had you come to work any later, you'd be fixing to leave for supper! But save me the excuses. I get the morning papers delivered to my very door up on Sherman. Have you ever read about that other total asshole called Don Quixote? He went in for saving the virtue of whores too, now that I study on it!"

Longarm flicked some tobacco ash on the rug, having heard that was hard on carpet mites and seeing no ashtray on his side of the desk, and soberly replied, "Miss Baltimore Barbara wasn't robbed of her virtue last night, Billy. She was robbed of her life, and speaking of book learning, have you ever read about that other total asshole, the Marquis de Sade? They had to lock *him* up to keep him from abusing gals like Baltimore Barbara, and *that* crazy bastard never really *killed* anybody!"

Vail grimaced, blew an octopus cloud of pungent smoke, and observed, "Carbonate Ned Cartier is not a prissy and long-dead Frenchman. He is a registered voter who votes the right way in Colorado, belongs to the mine owners' association of the same, and smelts forty ounces of silver from every ton of ore he drills, blasts, and mucks up Leadville way."

Longarm grimaced right back and replied, "Magnates such as Cartier don't drill, blast, or muck *shit*. The little folks do it *for* them, and they get to treating little folks like shit too. He *killed* that poor working gal, Billy. Threw her out a window like you'd throw an empty bottle or used condom if you were a real slob!"

Vail shrugged and said, "You got him to admit it, and the D.A. is so pleased with you he'd doubtless bend over and spread his cheeks. So how did you manage that, old son? I

14

know the papers *say* you confronted Cartier and his fibbing pal with the banged-up Baltimore Barbara, but that ain't possible. I asked. They tell me at the county coroner's she died of a busted neck and hasn't moved from that slab in the morgue since!''

Longarm nodded, blew a playful smoke ring, and asked, ''You remember that flea circus and museum of natural wonders on Larimer Street, Boss?''

Vail frowned and said, ''I do. They ought to be ashamed of themselves. Those fleas ain't trained. They're just stuck with glue to bitty toys and they pull them around as they try to get away.''

He scowled harder as he continued. ''As for the natural wonders in the back, they ain't half as natural as the fleas! I know for a fact they got this old drunk who was fired from a more famous wax museum back East. When he ain't under the table, he whips up all those two-headed critters, mermaid mummies, and such out of beeswax and that mashy paper they use for parade floats and such.''

Longarm nodded. ''I know old Abner better. One night I saved his hide from some meaner drunks when he was in no shape to fight a mean six-year-old. So he said he owed me, if ever I needed a mermaid or a two-headed crocodile. I didn't have any use for either. But last night I recalled how you get two heads that look as if they grew out of the same critter. You make a plaster cast of the one real head, and just mix up some beeswax, tinted the same color.''

''You never!'' Billy Vail shouted, grinning like a mean kid in spite of himself. ''How could you pass off a death mask as a real live gal, for Pete's sake?''

Longarm shrugged. ''Never had to, up close. Old Abner *means* well, but he ain't no Madame Tussaud. He just greased the dead gal's face as she grinned up from her slab, slathered her with plaster of Paris that sets in minutes, and meanwhile, Emma Gould and her own crew were mixing beeswax with face powder on a stove up front. The morgue attendants wouldn't let Abner cut any of the cadaver's real hair off. But once he'd pulled the cast and used it to make a mighty off-color but passible wax mask, old Emma and her maid, Willow, gussied up Frenching Ann with a head scarf sort of hiding where her own hair met the wax edges of her new face. Old Abner naturally had crutches and such on hand as well and, hell, what more do you need, a diagram on the blackboard?''

Vail chuckled but grumbled, ''You're going to need a field mission on the double, lest they serve you that summons before we can get you out of their reach!''

Longarm blinked and asked, ''Whose reach? The deal I made with the Denver P.D. was that I'd never be called before any Denver judge. They won't need my testimony. We tricked the killer into incriminating his fool self constitutionally, with neither the use of force or the threat of force.''

Vail snapped, ''Don't teach your granny to suck eggs or lecture this old lawman on the law! I ain't worried about you being called to the witness stand by the prosecution. Any lawyer worth his salt would surely call you as a witness for the defense!''

Longarm smiled incredulously. ''That's silly, Billy! I was nowhere near that whorehouse when Cartier killed that whore, and all I heard either him or his cellmate say was that he *done* it!''

Vail shook his bullet head and tried to sound like a high-toned lawyer. ''The jury has heard all about your Halloween prank on the defendant, Deputy Long. Now suppose you explain just why you went to so much trouble seeing you had no jurisdiction. Or was it because of your, ah, relationship with the notorious Emma Gould, the well-endowed Negress Willow Jones, and Frenching Ann? Why do they call her Frenching Ann, Deputy Long? I mean, seeing you seem to know her well enough to tear through the wee small hours playing Halloween pranks with spooky masks?''

Longarm stared aghast. ''Hold on! I never in my life had any such relationship as you're suggesting with any of them ladies! I was asked to help by Sergeant Nolan of the Denver P.D. Him and me go back a ways, ever since the two of us foiled a burglary at the Tabor mansion up on Capitol Hill.''

Vail sweetly asked in that fancy voice, "Is that why I can produce my own witnesses to the simple fact that you were traipsing up and down Larimer Street with notorious women of the town a good hour or more before you went anywhere near my client in his gloomy prison cell?''

Longarm blew smoke out both nostrils, but didn't paw the rug with a hoof as he quietly asked, "You said you had this field mission for me, Boss?''

Somewhat mollified, Vail nodded his bullet head and said, "They call him Wolf Ritter. His real name's Wolfgang von Ritterhoff, and before he come across the main ocean and turned total outlaw, he was one of those Prussian Cavalry johns who rode for Bismarck in that Franco-Prussian War a few years back. As the Austrians, Danes, and French could tell us, no Cheyenne Crooked Lancer could hold a candle to a Prussian trooper coming at you with a saber in one hand, a horse pistol in the other, and the reins gripped in his evil grin. But now that things are a tad calmer in that new Germanic Empire Bismarck carved out a few short years ago, such ferocious fighting men have been ordered to wax their pimp mustaches, click their heels on entering or leaving the ballroom, and in sum behave like officers and gentlemen.''

Longarm nodded thoughtfully. "Some old boys who rode in the war we had earlier have yet to adjust to civilian ways. I take it this Wolf Ritter never took too well to heel-clicking and kissing the ladies on their dainty wrists?''

Vail said, "Ritter hung on to his horse pistol, a LeMatt he took off a dead French officer at Sedan. It was kissing a lady of the Pawnee persuasion all over, against her will, that led to his being listed as a federal want. When the screaming Pawnee maiden's federal Indian agent tried to make Ritter stop, he wound up with nine rounds of .40-caliber and a modest load of buckshot in his guts. The Pawnee victim says the poor

17

gunshot cuss died slow and got to watch as Ritter finished what he'd set out to do to her. Any questions?''

Longarm quietly asked, ''Which way did he go?''

Vail said, ''South, to the Smokey Hill range north of Dodge. I had you over yonder on another case a spell back, remember?''

Longarm nodded. ''You damn near got me killed. But why in thunder would a total furriner choose that stretch of west Kansas to hide out in? I know you said he likes Indian gals. They're doubtless a change from Austrian, Danish, or French gals. But the South Cheyenne and Arapaho who used to range the Smokey Hill swells are long gone, and the country's been thrown open to stockmen and . . . Oh, I follow your drift!''

To which Vail replied, ''I was hoping you might. What do you call them High Dutch-speaking Russians who've come west to grow tumbleweeds and that red Russian wheat?''

Longarm said, ''Mennonites. They ain't exactly Russian. Catherine the Great, being a High Dutch princess to begin with, invited some unpopular but mighty good farmers to migrate to Russia with her and see what they could do with her back steps. That's what they call the prairies in Russia, steps.''

Vail said, ''Never mind all that. Is it or ain't it a fact that a mess of High Dutch Holy Rollers with beards and thick accents have infested the Smokey Hills of Kansas?''

Longarm nodded. ''Mennonites ain't Pentacostals inclined to speak in tongues and thrash about on the floor during services. From what a nice little gal told me a spell back, the main reason they got persecuted in their old countries was that they don't hold with baptizing their kids. That's why some call 'em Anabaptists. That ain't accurate, though. Their founding prophet, a Hollander named Menno, said babies didn't know whether they wanted to be Christians, Muslims, or hell, Hopi snake dancers when they grew up. So it was a lot more logical to let kids grow up and *then* baptize 'em, after they agreed to be Mennonites. But Mennonites call themselves Brethren when nobody else is around.''

18

Vail rolled his eyes up and groaned, "Ask the kid what time it might be and he lectures you on how to build a grandfather clock! I know all about those High Dutch Holy Rollers getting chased off those back steps by some other Russian emperor's cod-sacks, and how they didn't want to go back to that Germanic Empire because Bismarck had started to draft everybody into his spikey-hatted army. I know most of them settled in the Dakota Territory to pray their own way and raise all that red Russian wheat to their heart's content. The bunch that came down to Kansas to farm even tougher country are the ones Wolf Ritter seems to be hiding out with."

Longarm asked, "How come? As I understand it, Mennonites don't hold with violence, military or otherwise."

Vail said, "None of the simps would know a renegade Prussian officer if they caught him in bed with their woman, and as I'm sure Ritter was the first to notice, all those sod-busting Holy Rollers favor full beards as well as High Dutch accents!"

He saw that hadn't gotten through to Longarm and added, "Ritter went to that fancy military school where the students get to carve each other's faces with sabers when they ain't studying table manners. So he used to be mighty proud of his scarred-up left cheek. Such a distinctive feature on an otherwise average-looking face can be a bother when you're riding the owlhoot trail with many a murder warrant out after you."

Longarm said, "I follow your drift. I'm to look for a clodhopper with chin whiskers and a furrin accent, who's really a murderous vet of the Franco-Prussian War, among the Smokey Hills of Kansas, which are really rolling prairie carried to an extreme."

Vail said, "An informant who knows him on sight reported him last in a trail town called Sappa Crossing, a four or five days' ride north of Dodge City. I've already told Henry out front to route you by rail as far as the forks of the Republican River by way of the Burlington line. The ride south will be way shorter, and every time we let you get off in Dodge you seem to get stuck playing draw poker at that infernal Long

19

Branch, or playing slap and tickle with someone like Madame Mustache for at least a week!''

Longarm smiled innocently through the haze and quietly remarked, ''I ain't sure Madame Mustache still has that place in Dodge. Do you reckon on Wolf Ritter's dumb enough to be hanging on to that distinctive old LeMat revolver?''

Vail shrugged. ''Be dumb as hell to take such pains to hide out as a Holy Rolling homesteader without picking up a whole other gun. Either way, he'll likely be packing a concealed weapon, and the way I hear it, he's been trained to kill a heap with most any weapon handy!''

Chapter 4

Longarm got off the Burlington eastbound at the cow town of McCook, Nebraska, after he'd barely gotten started with that eastbound blonde in that low-cut summer frock. With nobody from the fussy home office looking, he'd shed his stuffy tweeds for a far more comfortable riding outfit of faded but soft clean denim jacket and jeans over a hickory work shirt. He'd learned on past missions, the hard way, it paid any man more interested in catching men than cows to stick with broken-in stovepipe boots he could ride or run in. His cross-draw .44-40 was a tad more noticeable without a frock coat to hide under, but nobody was likely to worry about a rider packing his hardware sensibly in plain leather wrapping.

Longarm's Winchester '73, chambered for the same .44-40 rounds as his double-action six-gun, naturally rode in a saddle boot attached to his McClellan army saddle, which, like his boots, reflected experience with unexpected experiences. General George McClellan had made a total hash of his Peninsula Campaign in '62, but before that he'd introduced one hell of a saddle, based on, but improved over, an Austro-Hungarian cavalry design he'd met up with during some diplomatic time in those parts. Old George's version rode easy on one's mount, with an open slit the length of the seat to ventilate the critter's spine and only grab you by the balls if you wore your riding pants too loose. Better yet, the McClellan saddle had brass eyelets you could hang a heap of shit from. So aside from his saddle gun and canteens, Longarm had that tweed suit, other spare duds, trail grub, and such packed in the two saddlebags riding under the bedroll behind the cantle. It made quite a load as he limped across the dusty street from the train stop with all of it balanced on one hip. He had no need to make the usual courtesy call on the local law, seeing he'd be clean out of the state as well as the county by nightfall. So that might have been why the old boys watching from around the livery corral on the far side added two and two to get half a dozen.

When Longarm draped his heavy saddle over a corral pole and asked them about the hire of a pony, a gray old gent with a hatchet face spat ominously close to Longarm's dusty boot tips and allowed they had no horses for hire to the likes of him.

There came a murmured growl of agreement from the eight others assembled, all dressed cow and no fancier than himself. So Longarm quietly replied, "Sure you do. That sign on the side of your whitewashed stable allows you hire livery for hauling or riding at two bits a head per diem with deposit. After that, I can plainly see at least six or eight head of horseflesh in that corral behind you. So what's your personal beef with me, old son?"

The hostler said, "It ain't you personal. It's your kind in general. I wouldn't hire to Johnny Ringo, Billy the Kid, or any other wandering gunslick, if that's any comfort to you."

Longarm laughed and reached for his wallet as he sheepishly said, "That'll learn me to pack guns in public without a suit and tie. I thought President Hayes was just being a priss when he ordered all of us to dress like whiskey drummers."

By this time he had his wallet out to flash his badge and identification for all to see. The hostler gasped. "Great balls of fire! You must be that Deputy Long from Denver they call Longarm! We knew someone like you would be coming along

22

sooner or later! How many horses do you need—on the house, Longarm?''

The denim-clad deputy put his wallet away as he chuckled and said he only needed one to ride and one for packing. Then he added, ''I'd be proud to pay your going price. It don't come out of my pocket. Not directly leastways. We all pay taxes. How come you gents here in McCook seem so proddy about gunslicks? I ain't heard about any recent gunplay in these parts.''

The hostler took a throw-rope from a nail near a gatepost, swung the gate ajar, and a said, ''Come on in and point out the ones you want. You ain't heard about the shooting because the shooting ain't started so far.''

Longarm pointed with his chin at a wary-eyed but not too spooked gelding and said, ''That cut bay neither dances nor drags his hooves in the dust. How come you're expecting shooting if there ain't been any?''

The hostler threw with considerable skill, gently caught the bay on the first try, and rolled him in slow but steady as he explained. ''The reason me and the boys started out so surly was because you ain't the first armed and dangerous-looking stranger to get off a train passing through such a normally quiet town. The spring roundup just ended. So our local cow outfits are more likely to be laying off than hiring and, no offense, none of you recent arrivals look like plow jockies, even if our newer homesteaders were busting new sod, which they ain't.''

As the two of them got the bay gelding against the rails to saddle and bridle him, Longarm betrayed more of his West-by-God-Virginia boyhood than his Colorado-crushed Stetson might be letting on when he said, ''You're right. This late in the greenup all the spring planting's been done, and it's too early to reap last fall's winter wheat. So what's left?''

One of the other old boys who'd started listening chimed in with, ''Nothing. The buff have been shot off in these parts, and we ain't never had no mines or mills for old boys to work

23

in. The range north and south or east and west is stock and farming country for many a mile. Some say it's a range war brewing. Ain't nothing else worth fighting over in these parts. Yet some damned somebody has invited a whole lot of hired guns to get off here!''

Longarm pointed at another steady-looking pony and said, ''I like the way all four hooves of that paint mare match. I've yet to hear of a war over water rights this close to the Smokey Hills.''

The hostler shook out another loop as he replied, ''It can't be over water. The last month's been dry, after a wet enough spring. But hell, it's always dry out here on these prairies in summertime. Otherwise we'd be surrounded by forests. But even when the creeks run dry, a settler with a lick of sense would rather drill for water than fight a neighbor along that same dry creek.''

He threw, and again made an easy, clean catch. As he was getting a tad more resistance from the paint, the old boy leaning over the corral pole at them volunteered, ''Water table's always high in these parts. I can't see a water fight neither. Ain't no cows been getting stole or fences being cut. Country ain't that settled yet. Of course, some of us real Americans can't abide by them Minuets down the far side of Sappa Creek.''

As the hostler got the paint mare to the rails and Longarm calmed her with a bandana blindfold and a horsehair hackamore or soft bitless bridle, he felt obliged to observe, ''Sappa Creek's a good ride from here, and I understand you call them Mennonites. I know that much because I'm headed for Sappa Crossing, Lord willing and the creeks don't rise. I understand I got more than one to cross betwixt here and yonder.''

The hostler thought and decided, ''Mostly bitty draws and, like Lem just said, it's been dry all month. Only one you'll likely find with enough flowing water to matter will be Beaver Creek, this side of the somewhat wetter Sappa. You're right about wells. Most every natural homesteader out this way

24

prays for rain and drills for water. Save for them peculiar Anabaptists south of Sappa Creek.''

As he and the hostler got a hired empty packsaddle on the paint Longarm resisted the impulse to ask what was so peculiar about the Mennonite nesters to the south. The loafer called Lem volunteered. ''They do ever'thing bass-ackwards. They wait till their kids are full growed and out of most dangerous stages before they baptize 'em to insure their souls. And they plow and plant in the *fall*, when all the sensible folk are *reaping*. So damned if they don't pray for *snow* instead of *rain*, just as that crazy red wheat is commencing to sprout!''

Longarm knew better. He still said quietly, ''That's how come they call it winter wheat. The Mennonites met up with it on the back steps of Russia where the growing season's even shorter than out our way. It sprouts before Yuletide, like you said, but as soon as the wolf winds nip, winter wheat dies above ground, goes dormant underground, and the process repeats through all the frosts and thaws until the stuff really gets to growing in the first real thaws in April, when nobody but a fool would try to plow shin-deep prairie muck.''

The hostler cracked the gate open. As they led the two ponies out, a couple of old boys with nothing better to do dropped down off the rails to shoo the other livery stock back with their hats. Country gents weren't really as mean as they talked when they didn't know you.

Lem, who hadn't pitched in to help, spat and said, ''It ain't so smart to bust this sod at any time of the year. Most of the time it's dried to 'dobe hard as chalk, and on the rare occasions it's wet, it turns to gumbo, like you said. There's barely enough time in a good year to grow a cash crop of barley for piss-poor cash. That's why I grow cows, like most of the other real Americans in these parts!''

There came a rumble of agreement as Longarm settled up with the hostler, ticked his hat brim to all concerned, and led the two ponies away afoot. He wasn't ready to ride just yet.

He passed the saloon just up the street, and tethered his

25

livery stock to the hitching rail of a nearby general store. He had a few cans of beans and tomato preserves in one saddlebag. But seeing he had some riding ahead through nester country in tenser times than old Billy Vail had warned him about, he figured some extra private fodder for the ponies might save discussion on possibly disputed range.

As the fatherly old storekeeper and a colored kid filled his order for cracked corn and rolled oats, the kid getting to carry the sacks out and load them aboard the paint, Longarm stocked up on some extra tobacco, canned coffee, and rock candy. You couldn't just hand out smokes to the menfolk as you rode through farming country.

He settled up with the storekeeper. But the older gent followed him out front, nodded with approval at the stock of Longarm's saddle gun, and suggested, "Don't take no guff off them Anabaptist bastards down Kansas way. They act big. But none of 'em stand ready to fight a grown man or, hell, a tough Christian girl!"

Longarm tipped the kid helper a whole dime to show he wasn't in a huff as he mounted up and rode out of town to the south. Nobody had told him things were that tense in these parts, and a High Dutch-talking killer made more sense when you considered nobody had much respect for the fighting ability of those High Dutch newcomers. The prophet, Menno, had preached against fighting and advised the Brethren to turn the other cheek. Longarm had heard much the same in his own Sunday School, in times that now seemed long ago and far more peaceful. But he'd noticed, out West, that that was a swell way to get slapped twice.

As he left the last outhouse in McCook behind, he saw newly sprouted corn and what had to be either rye or barley behind the three-strand fencing to either side of the dusty wagon trace. Corn called for a heap of optimisim west of Longitude 100° between the Arkansas and Republican, while spring wheat was just plain impossible. If that old Lem had been right about cows in these parts as well, those three strands

26

weren't enough. It took at least five strands of bob-wire, stapled to solid posts, to stop a determined cow.

He had no call to tell anybody any of these things, so he kept on riding. He'd been raised country enough to know most country folks got smart about the sort of country they were used to, making them scornful of book learning and resentful of strangers offering advice about their own damned business.

Left to their druthers and doing things their own ways, country folks tended to get along just fine on the folklore handed down and slowly modified when anything wasn't exactly as the grandfolks had said it ought to be. Old country tales about Cock Robin showing up just before the spring thaw worked just as well if the robins of a new land were a different bird entirely, and it still rained, sooner or later, after you stomped on a spider.

It was throwing together all sorts of country folks from different countries, with different ways, that led to so much feuding and failures in the postwar West. Some, like Longarm, had soon learned the earth would not gape open and swallow them if they listened to odd-sounding advice from folks who'd been out West longer, or even paid attention to a Mexican or full-blown Indian. The old ways your grandfolks taught you could lead to heartbreak or worse in totally different country.

The first pioneers who'd jeered at Indian warnings about what seemed to be wild parsley, free for the taking near camp, had wound up deader than the ones who'd kept more open minds.

Texas stockmen had lost cows left and right to agues and weeds no Anglo had ever met up with before, until some few had been politer to those outlandish Mex *vaqueros* and learned to be Texas buckaroos almost overnight.

That Homestead Act of old Abe Lincoln had killed far more folks than all the hostile Indians combined, and busted far more folks than it killed. But Longarm had learned in his travels how tough it could be to convince farmers from the wet side of the Mississippi that a hundred sixty acres and pure

27

sweat alone weren't always going to be enough, that an old hand worried more about grasshoppers than Cheyenne raids and that your stove did better on dry cowshit than almost worthless cottonwood a couple of draws over.

He knew the *resentment* at the way this new country could treat a willing worker added fuel to the fire when some outlandish stranger sneered at you for doing things the wrong way. it was easier to sneer back or perhaps peg a shot at the bastard than it was to allow you'd been dumb to follow the ways of your elders that had always worked before.

As he lit a cheroot with a passing nod at a scarecrow pointing the way to the nearby state line, Longarm reflected on the many American-born homesteaders who *had* started switching from regular spring wheat to red Russian or other winter wheats of late. For the Mennonites had been growing wheat west of where wheat was supposed to grow for close to five summers by now. It was the stubborn old-timers who refused to consider changing who could be your most surly neighbors.

Longarm, who'd taken up reading as a secret vice in recent years, had read how country folks in olden times had charged neighbors more prosperous with witchcraft. A poor Ohio Valley sodbuster watching a funny-talking cuss reaping bumper crops of red wheat after he'd tried, and failed, more than once, could almost be forgiven for feeling moody and suspicious, if willful ignorance had been an excuse. It wasn't, but it still had to hurt like fire to plant the same wheat your ever-so-great grandad had planted, once the prairie was dry enough for spring planting, only to see the dry winds of a high plains summer turn half of it to straw before the early fall frosts finished it off before it was ripe enough to reap.

The wagon trace was taking him gently but firmly skyward as he and the two ponies forged on to the south. So he wasn't surprised to find ever more open range all around, until they had widely scattered cows on overgrazed short grass for company. Mindful of the grade and his own bigger frame, Longarm dismounted sooner than he might have to lead the ponies aside to crop grass while he swapped saddles. Despite being grazed too heavily, the grass was still growing and fairly green. The dry winds across these rises would soon summer-kill and cure it. A crop down closer to the riverbanks north or south might make it a few weeks further into high summer without irrigation, but not enough to matter, unless it was bar-ley. Corn and rye both needed extra watering out this way. None of them sold for as much as good bread-wheat. Mount-ing the paint so the bay could pack the lighter load for a spell, Longarm nodded to a chongo-horned cow who'd been watch-ing with interest and told it, "Your owner's right. If *I* was stuck with a few sections of this range, I'd leave it to short grass and run your kind on it."

Then he told himself nobody had stuck him with one acre over in these parts, and got out the onionskins Henry had typed up for him to worry about. He'd read them more than once aboard the Burlington eastbound, but you never knew what you might notice reading the same reports over again. So far, they hadn't told him a whole lot.

On the face of the odd tale, the fugitive Wolf Ritter had gone to ground among High Dutch-speakers who wore beards along the south bank of Sappa Creek. The only trouble with that was how a Prussian *von* was supposed to pass for a Men-nonite from the back steps of Russia. That friendly Mennonite gal who'd explained the whole sad saga to him a spell back had allowed her folks spoke a sort of Swiss Dutch, before picking up some Russian words in the hundred years or so they'd spent as subjects of various czars. A renegade but high-born Prussian officer might manage the accent well enough to fool anyone but a real Mennonite, the way a Boston boy might try to sound as if he hailed from Dixie. But someone from, say, Mobile was likely to trip him up sooner or later.

"That might account for our informant spotting him," Longarm told his paint mount as he saw that the informant was a Mennonite by the name of Horst Heger, according to Henry's typing. Longarm wished the infernal report had more

to say about the informant than the son of a bitch he'd in-
formed on. There was no mystery about the disgusting ways
of Wolf Ritter, né von Ritterhoff, since he'd fought one duel
too many in his old country and started picking fights as soon
as he got off the boat in New York City. Aside from that one
federal killing, he was wanted for manslaughter or assault all
along a route you could trace through upstate New York and
the Midwest and beyond, as if that hot-tempered scar-faced
rascal was riding with Mister Death into the sunset, the way
some held they'd seen that dark rider on a pale horse after
Shiloh, Cold Harbor, and such.

So how had a Mennonite farmer who'd never been in any
Prussian army recognized Ritter as Ritter?

The report didn't say. Longarm's orders were to get on
down to Sappa Crossing, scout up Horst Heger, and ask him
to point Ritter out from the other bearded gents.

Without flushing a short-fused owlhoot rider who knew the
law had to be out to hang him high!

That was the rub nothing in these fool onionskins offered a
lick of advice on. Oh, sure, Henry had typed plain as day,
"SUSPECT IS ARMED AND EXTREMELY DANGER-
OUS!" as if a body had to be told a killer packing a LeMat
with nine in the wheel and a shotgun shell in the center of it
was likely to roll over and beg you to scratch his belly.

Snorting smoke out both nostrils, Longarm cursed and told
his mount, "That there Horst Heger must have *some* plan."
Had Wolf Ritter suspected anyone was on to him, Billy never
would have got that wire. A killer desperate enough to grow
a beard and take up new religious ways would swat anyone
he suspected like a fly. Heger had been smart enough to send
his fifty-word night letter from the county seat a half-day's
drive away from Sappa Crossing. But fifty words were hardly
enough. Henry had typed up a full transcription of the tersely
worded message to Marshal Vail. Longarm had read it over
before and as he read it again, walking his ponies, he failed
to see anything he might have missed riding east on that train.

30

The informant who'd recognized a Prussian killer hadn't seen fit to explain why he'd wired Denver instead of the much closer federal court at Fort Dodge. He said the man he knew as von Ritterhoff had come into his shop in Sappa Crossing. He never said what sort of a shop he ran or exactly where it was. So for openers, a stranger who could well be the law had to ask around town for Horst Heger and hope like hell he wasn't asking Wolf Ritter in disguise!

Longarm had already considered trying to blend in with a bunch of Dutch-Russian Anabaptists, and given up the notion as silly. Mennonites didn't attach any religious significance to clothes or personal grooming, the way those Pennsylvania Dutch did. But most of them looked sort of outlandish because they *were* outlandish, more used to dressing like Russian peasants than American homesteaders. Some of the younger ones he'd met had taken to dressing and shaving more naturally. Their elders seemed an easygoing bunch next to, say, the Latter-Day Saints or even the Hard Shell Baptists. So a gent riding in discreetly in faded denim and with his guns out of sight . . .

"Forget it," Longarm warned himself with a wry smile. "You talk a lot more Spanish that High Dutch, and you'd never in this world pass for a Mex if you put on a silly hat! As to your side arm, you'll be up against an experienced duelist who could be packing a nine-shooter when and if you meet, and folks in a small trail town are surely going to spot and speculate on anyone riding in day, night, or sideways!"

So he'd have to make up some excuse for a U.S. deputy marshal being there when he made the expected courtesy call on the town law. An armed and dangerous-looking stranger who went poking about town as a total mystery was as likely to be backshot by a proddy town deputy as the son of a bitch he was prodding for.

Longarm hummed a few bars of "Farther Along" as he decided he could make up some other outlaw he was after by the time he got to Sappa Crossing. And he could likely find a

31

barber, even in a town where so many favored beards, and just casually ask where old Heger's shop was. It seemed highly unlikely a trail-town barber would be the one and original Wolf Ritter.

Once he found Heger's shop, he'd just ask the shopkeeper when and where he'd met up with that mean Prussian. It hardly seemed likely any gent who'd turned Ritter in to the law would hold anything back about him.

Chapter 5

South central Nebraska and northwest Kansas shared the same rolling sea of short grass. So there was just no saying where that wagon trace crossed the state line. Up close, the country was less tedious to look at than it seemed from a train window. As the U.S. Cav had learned the hard way, back when this had been Arapaho and Cheyenne hunting ground, what seemed a view across open prairie to the far and flat horizon was dissected by draws deep enough to hide whole Indan villages, guarded by the best light cavalry on Earth. The winds that swept mostly from the west but constantly from any direction made it a mite tough for anything taller than buffalo and grama grass or widely scattered clumps of soap weed to occupy the rises. But the deeper draws could surprise you with long skinny forests of box elder, cottonwood, willow, and even small red cedars. The buffalo had been shot off this far east, along with the buffalo-hunting Indians, but prairie dogs still cussed at you on high ground, and jackrabbits flushed to spook your ponies most anywhere.

Longarm had left McCook a tad later than an easy day's ride down to Sappa Crossing called for. So even though he knew it was *possible* to push on and arrive by moonrise, that would hardly be the way to drift into a tight-knit little trail town without everyone in town hearing about it within the hour.

His government survey map showed a regular American trail town named Cedar Bend, where the wagon trace crossed Beaver Creek a few hours north of his Mennonite destination.

Longarm decided he might kill more than one bird with the same slowpoke stone if he overnighted there and rode on into tenser parts in the morning, when traffic would be busier on the roads.

Horst Heger hadn't sent that wire from Cedar Bend, so the wanted killer would have no call to be watching for one particular rider in a regular American settlement.

At the same time, the two towns were close enough to one another for any important news to travel back and forth. They'd have surely heard up ahead if there'd been any gunplay in Sappa Crossing since that Burlington eastbound had pulled out of Denver. In a land where your nearest neighbor could be over the horizon, miles could be little more than city blocks to the local gossips.

Putting his map away, Longarm saw he had no call to consult his watch. The sun shone well above the western horizon in a clear cobalt-blue sky, and he knew Cedar Bend lay just over the next serious rise to his south. So he clucked the bay he was riding now into an easy lope, leading the paint at the same pace downslope and across a grassy draw, to rein in and walk both ponies up the long grassy grade ahead.

As he did so, gazing ahead at the crest of the rise they were climbing, Longarm muttered, "What the hell . . . ?" as what seemed like a big old pumpkin peeked over the rise at them and continued skyward at a rate that would have done an eagle-bird proud.

"Why, it's a swamping balloon!" Longarm assured his mount as he made out the spiderwebby line following the big yellow globe skyward. "It's a *captive* balloon, being flown like a kite by someone on the ground with a mighty expensive hobby! Those hydrogen-generating wagons cost a heap, and the scrap iron and sulfuric acid you have to fill 'em up with don't come all that cheap!''

He heeled his mount into a faster uphill walk as he thought back to all that the pretty Mam-zell Blanchard had taught him about ballooning, and other French notions, at the Omaha State Fair. They'd met up there because it took something as big as a state fair to finance the sort of ballooning stunts he'd learned from her. His survey figures for Cedar Bend didn't list four hundred permanent residents, and even when you counted cowhands and nesters from all around, the only way anyone could profit from a captive balloon just hanging around up yonder would be to charge each passenger quite a lot per ride.

But as he peered heavenward, Longarm failed to see any passengers or even a sensible passenger basket under that big balloon. He'd just asked his mount's opinion on what that all meant when they both had the liver and lights scared out of them.

The box dangling from under the mighty high balloon blew up with a blinding flash, followed shortly thereafter by a horrendous bang and rumbling echoes from the rises all around. So it was a good thing Longarm had been aboard a bucking bronc before.

There was no horn on a McClellan saddle to grab onto. So Longarm let go of the lead rope and hung on to the saddlebow for dear life as the spooked pony crow-hopped all the way back to the bottom of the draw.

By that time the echoes had faded, he had his mount under control again and, as he'd hoped, the paint had not seen fit to carry that packsaddle up out of the draw towards such a noisy sky.

As he swung down to retrieve the lead line, he told both ponies in a soothing tone, ''Nobody's out to bombard us. Some fool *pluviculturist* is trying to make it rain. I just read in the *Scientific American* how some jasper called Dan'l Ruggles just *patented* what happened up yonder.''

Neither pony argued about that. As the three of them headed

35

back up the same slope, Longarm saw that same balloon still floating a whole lot higher, and idly wondered if he was fixing to meet the famous Rainmaking Ruggles. His picture in that magazine had doubtless been posed for on a bad day. The poor bewhiskered cuss in the stovepipe hat had looked as if his invention had scared him shitless.

The notion of setting off dynamite in the sky to make it rain had hardly been the basis of the Ruggles patent, of course. Folks as far back as the first Napoleon had noticed that all those cannon going off made for wetter weather than usual. Soldiers even further back had cussed about "General Mudd" slowing down their wars. So a gent by the name of James Espy had decided it was the smoke and heat above a battlefield that made such places so muddy. But his plan to water Penn State by burning big bonfires clean across the state, all at once, hadn't struck anyone as practical before the war.

Lots of war vets had come home in blue or gray to bitterly remark on all the damned mud they'd had to march through as the drizzle wet their damned powder. So a Texan named Dyrenforth had piled up enough explosives to start the war over and blasted hell out of the dry Texas skies till a dry Texas newspaper reported, "General Dyrenforth attacked front and rear, by the right and left flank. But the blue sky remained clear as the complexion of a Saxon maid!"

Ruggles's new patent involved getting the explosives up high in the sky where it might matter, without losing an expensive kite or balloon in the process. The scientific pluviculturist dangled his explosives a safe distance below the balloon on a lighter line branching off from the main one. Two copper wires were braided up yonder with three strands of hemp, so a simple charge from a blasting box could detonate the dangling dynamite at will.

So far this afternoon it didn't seem to be raining. The dark smoke had drifted away on the high breezes, and there didn't seem to be another whiff of cloud in that mighty arid-looking sky.

"That's likely why they're paying to have their summer sky shaken a mite," Longarm muttered with a thin smile as he forged on up over the rise.

Then he reined in near a fence post beside the wagon trace, regarded the view to the south, and murmured aloud, "Now, ain't that sort of pretty!"

Some cowboys and most Indians would have disagreed, but Longarm had to admire hard work and the fruits of the same. He saw no cedars where a cluster of frame structures faced him on the far side of a gentle bend in Beaver Creek. For that matter he saw no beavers, and there was hardly enough water running along the braided sandy channel to justify the title of Creek.

They'd built at such a respectful height up the far slope to show that when it *was* raining in the Smokey Hills to the southwest, you got more of a river than any creek around that bend. There was nothing in the way of a bridge across Beaver Creek. You didn't need bridges to cross such prairie watercourses in dry weather, and in wet weather any bridge you might build tended to wash out. They still spoke in awe up in Denver about the time a flash flood in Cherry Creek had picked up the Larimer Street Bridge and just wiped away some of Downtown Denver, like the thunderbird had been cleaning a blackboard with a big old eraser.

Some friendly Arapaho had tried to warn the founding fathers of Denver about Cherry Creek. Longarm was inclined to agree with the folks even other Indians called "The Grandfather Nation" that the best way to get along with their Ma'tou or Great Medicine was to ride it with a gentle hand on the reins. The folks of Cedar Bend had been smart enough to build above the high-water mark down yonder. Whether you got rain in the right amount by setting off bombs in the sky was another matter.

They seemed to be reeling that balloon back down toward an ant-pile scurry of distant folks on the far side of the valley. Whether anyone yonder knew his ass from his elbow remained to be seen. It was easier to see why they'd hired somebody to try.

The fenced-in forty acres of barley to his left looked sort of dry, but it was starting to head up and they'd likely fetch a crop on such ground water as the thrifty barley roots could still reach. As he heeled his hired bay downslope he saw other barley and a big patch of rye on the same southward-facing slope. Over yonder, facing north, he saw many more acres planted to flint corn, which was about shoulder high so far.

You planted hardy flint corn this far out on the high plains, even though an Eastern farmer's first thoughts would be against it. But while it was true the north slopes of prairie rises caught pure frozen hell in wintertime out this way, the warmer and drier south slopes were cruel to corn in summertime. You could barely hope to grow barley or rye where the sun and summer south winds could hit full blast.

That balloon was about down now and sure enough, he could make out a couple of big red circus-style wagons over yonder. A lot of that corn to his south had been planted low enough for irrigation, if those tall sunflower windmills along the far edge of town meant anything. But as was ever the temptation of mankind, some of that corn and a lot more barley had been drilled in halfway up the far slope. So they had to hope, pray, or pluviculture some rain soon. That mild moist greenup they'd had this year, after the long dry spell after Little Big Horn, had encouraged some nesters to gamble. He could tell from his side of the valley that some homesteaders had planted upslope from that line of windmills and other improvements above the town. Stockmen were inclined to range their critters far beyond any official holdings as well. But while you could always move a thirsty critter to such water as there might be, a corn stalk just stood there until either you got some damned water to it or it withered up and blew away.

"It ain't our problem," he told his mount as they got to the mostly sandy bed of Beaver Creek and crossed it, with neither pony wetting a hoof to the fetlock. He didn't say Billy Vail had sent him to cut the trail of Wolf Ritter. Not out loud. For an old gray geezer wearing an old army shirt with a snuff-colored vest and a Schofield .45-28 in a tie-down holster seemed to be regarding him with bemused interest as he rode up the far bank.

"Welcome to Cedar Bend and let me tell you about our pistol ordinance," the old-timer began. But Longarm got out his own badge so he could flash it without saying much. This inspired the older lawman to snort, "*Keep* your durned guns for all I care, Uncle Sam. You had a body worried, scouting a spell up yonder, before you rode down to hit town from this side with everyone else up the other way watching them fool rainmaking gals."

As Longarm reined and dismounted he put his badge away and introduced himself by name, adding, "Rainmaking *gals*? Not the one and pure patent holder, Dan'l Ruggles?"

The old-timer replied, "They call me Dad Jergens, and I do believe them rainmaking gals call themselves the Ruggles sisters, now that I think back. If it was up to me I'd run 'em out of town as pure public pests. But the town council said to give 'em a crack at making it rain. We need some rain. But I don't believe in rainmaking, do you?"

Longarm shrugged and replied, "Haven't seen it work yet. Spent a tedious seventy-two hours in a Hopi pueblo with rain-makers one time. It hadn't rained by the time I left, despite all that drumming and a whole lot of snake dancing. Where can I bed down these ponies for the night, Dad? I can tell you on the way why I figure I ought to stay here instead of riding into Sappa Crossing after sundown."

The old-timer said, "I'll show you the way to our municipal corral. They don't charge extra for watering stock, but fodder will run you a dime a head for corn and hay or an extra nickel for oats. I know why you don't want to hit that Anabaptist town after dark. You just now made *me* wonder, and I'm a sensible Methodist."

"You did seem a mite on the prod," said Longarm as they strode side by side to higher ground along the combined wagon trace and main street. He didn't have to ask why. The older lawman nodded and said, "Outlaws. Robbery over to the county seat and mayhaps a kidnapping or more down to Sappa Crossing!"

Longarm whistled softly and, taking the bull by the horns, told the other lawman, "I was supposed to look up some Mennonite shopkeeper down yonder. Is it understood this conversation is a private one, betwixt professional lawmen?"

Dad Jergens snorted, "Aw, hell, let me in on some secrets so's I can mount the pulpit at First Methodist come Sunday and preach 'em to the world! Have you any notion at all what a lawman worth his salt has to keep to himself in your average election year, old son?"

Longarm nodded and said, "The brother's name is Horst Heger. All I know about him is that he's supposed to have some sort of shop down in that Mennonite settlement."

Dad Jergens shook his head and said, "I know him. He's all right. I ride over yonder from time to time to do business with Heger. He's a gunsmith. A good one. Fixed this old cavalry iron of mine to shoot straight as ever after I'd pistolwhupped a chicken thief with more enthusiasm than Major Schofield had in mind when he designed it for shooting Indians. Hold the thought and we'll talk about Heger some more, in private."

The figure coming out of the stable next to the municipal corral appeared to be an Indian, baby-faced and walking effeminately until it became more obvious you were staring at a handsome pair of tits under that red shirt and bib overalls. It sure beat all how a face could look so wrong on a young buck and so right on a young squaw with the same long parted and braided hair. Longarm noticed that aside from dressing like a white stable hand, the gal hadn't painted the part of her hair any medicine color. So he had her down as an assimilate well before Dad Jergens said, "Deputy Long, this here would

40

be Osage Olive and she's all right, despite her savage appearance.''

The squaw, who'd have doubtless preferred to be called a *weya* if she spoke Osage, smiled wearily at the old-timer and told Longarm she answered to Olive Red-Dog.

He thought hard and tried, ''That'd be Miss Sunka Luta then, right?''

The Indian gal's sloe eyes betrayed no emotion, but she dimpled some as she replied, ''I think I know who you must be. There is this Deputy Long called Longarm by his own people. My people call him the Wasichu Wastey. That means he is one of them who's all right.''

Longarm dryly asked if that meant he didn't have to pay extra for oats. Olive Red-Dog laughed as hearty as a boy.

Dad Jergens said, ''Well, you kids go on and rub down them ponies or one another for all I care. I got to get on over to that rainmaking operation before real trouble starts in these parts.''

''Hold on, we were talking about gunsmiths!'' Longarm called after the spry older lawman as Jergens lit out at a mile-eating pace.

The Indian gal reached for the reins and lead line Longarm was holding as she suggested, ''Go after him, if it's important. Dad's all right but he's a tad deaf as well as absentminded.''

When Longarm hesistated, as any thoughtful rider would have, Olive said, ''This may come as a surprise to you, Wasichu Wastey, but I make my living tending to horses. You'll find your saddle and possibles in the tack room when you come back to settle up. It's those Cheyenne who count coup on robbing you boys. My people were on your side, back when things were wilder in these parts, remember?''

Longarm surrendered his riding stock to her with a smile, saying, ''I was counting coup further east, at places such as Shiloh and Cold Harbor. Could you tell me what your town law is so exited about this afternoon, Miss Olive?''

She nodded and replied, ''Those rainmaking Wasichu girls.

41

I don't think they're going to make it rain. But some have paid good money for some much-needed sky-water, while those wheat farmers down the other side of the Sappa have threatened bodily harm to anyone fixing to dampen their ripening crops with a heavy dew before they can reap it, standing proud in dry fields.''

Longarm rolled his eyes heavenward and tore after the town law, shouting, ''Wait for me, you anxious cuss!''

Chapter 6

Longarm caught up with Dad Jergens a furlong up a narrow side street, fell in beside him, and mildly observed, "I seem to be missing a detail or more. First you tell me those turn-the-other-cheek Mennonites support their friendly neighborhood gunsmith, and now Olive Red-Dog has them threatening rainmakers with *violence*?"

Dad Jergens replied, "Oh, there you are. Thought I'd lost you for a minute there. I *asked* Horst Heger about selling guns to such a flock of doves when I got him to fix my Schofield. He said they ain't as set in their ways about guns as them Pennsylvania Dutch, and even some of *them* hold with hunting for the pot or shooting a weasel in the chicken coop. Mennonites are agin' marching as to war. Their faith allows for self-defense, within reason."

Longarm demanded, "Including the assassination of ignorant water witches who think they're being scientific?"

To which Dad Jergens simply replied, "Some of them Dutch-Rooshin sodbusters are sort of ignorant in their own right. Them Ruggles gals claim they have a U.S. patent on their noisy method, with magazine and newspaper clippings in a big old scrapbook to back their brag."

Longarm snorted in digust and said, "That patent, if it's

theirs to begin with, is on a method of setting off explosives carried aloft by a balloon without losing the balloon. There may or may not be something to setting off charges inside a brooding rain cloud. Detonating dynamite in a clear sunny sky, low enough to impress the folks on the ground at lower cost, is what the alienists who study the peculiar call 'sympathetic magic.' That's where you treat snakebite by biting a snake, get your trees to bear more fruit by holding an orgy in the orchard, or curdle an enemy's milk by pouring vinegar in some of you own, with his name written on the jar.''

Dad Jergens shrugged and said, ''I heard beating the trunks of fruit trees works. What's so sympathetic about setting off bombs in the sky?''

Longarm snorted in disgust and replied, ''It sounds like thunder, and everyone but old Ben Franklin used to know how thunder brought on rain. It was wise old Ben, way back when we still had a king and queen, who proved scientifically that first it starts to rain, and then the rain falling through the clouds builds up this electic charge you need for thunder and lightning. Big chemical bangs up yonder are as likely to bring on rain as buying a gal a box of chocolates and eating it youself is likely to make her fall in love with you!''

They could see the top of that orange balloon above the rooftops ahead now. Hauled down to ground level, it looked big as hell. Dad Jergens said, ''I hope you're right about it being a heap of horseshit. I can handle our own disgruntled Methodists, Baptists, and such. Them rainmaking gals offer a money-back guarantee, and I warned 'em what I'd do if they tried skipping out with the money along a dusty road. But I ain't sure each and every Mennonite would listen to me, or anybody, if the Ruggles sisters managed a good gullywasher just as they were fixing to haul their mighty McCormick reapers over firm fields rapidy turning to gumbo.''

Longarm whistled softly. ''Lord have mercy, they've drilled in enough of that red Russian wheat to rate mechanical reaping?''

The old-timer said, "Turkish red. Some of our boys asked where they got such wondrous seed. They said they'd tried all sorts of winter wheat for their czars, and settled on this one strain the Turks to the south did well with. Some of our boys are of a mind to try it, crazy as it sounds to plow and plant in fall with a blizzard likely to blow in any minute. You're sure those Ruggles gals ain't likely to make it rain? The way I hear tell, that red winter wheat down Sappa Crossing way has made a bumper crop this year thanks to that early wet spring and all this dry summer sunshine."

As if to argue that very point, the big balloon ahead shot skyward again on its braided line, a pasteboard box about right for a pair of new Justins dangling about thirty feet under the gas bag against the eastern sky that was now sort of lavender. As the rays of the low western sun caught the balloon broadside, it seemed to light up like a Japanese paper lantern. Fakes or not, those mysterious Ruggles sisters knew a thing or two about putting on a show.

Dad Jergens seemed to think so too. Striding faster, he moaned aloud, "Damn their sassy hides, they told me they only meant to set off that last blast!"

Picking up his own pace, Longarm said, "It ain't fixing to rain no matter what they might do! There ain't enough clouds for a beautiful sunset this evening, and we were talking about bank robberies, kidnappings, and a Mennonite gunsmith named Horst Heger, remember?"

Dad Jergens replied, "Heger ain't one of them Dutch-Rooshins. His wife and a mess of in-laws are. He told me one time he hailed from Berlin Town, and studied on guns in that Prussian Army under Bismarck. Said them Prussian needle guns sure shot the shit outten the French in that war they had."

Longarm scowled thoughtfully up at the rapidly rising balloon ahead. "Stranger flimflams have been pulled on this child. So could you tell me whether Horst Heger sports a dueling scar on his left jaw, or a beard that might be hiding it?"

Dad Jergens shook his head. "Wrong both times. Has one

of them pointy waxed mustaches Bismarck's boys go in for, but both cheeks are smooth shaven. All the time. He says he used to be an officer and he's a bit of a dandy about it.''

Longarm didn't answer aloud as he told himself an ex-Prussian officer recognizing a renegade Prussian officer made more sense than a wanted killer wiring in his current whereabouts. But if Heger was still looking like his old self, how come Wolf Ritter hadn't recognized *him*? Or had a killer on the dodge been just as slick and kept such thoughts to himself for later?

The two lawmen broke out into the open, east of the last housing, to join a good-sized crowd for such a town as, up above, that orange balloon rose ever higher with the low western sun gilding it brightly against that clear darkening sky. A wishing star had just winked on over to the east. It was easy to guess what most of the corn planters for miles were wishing for.

As Longarm followed the older lawman's elbowing progress through the crowd, they came to where a single-strand rope barrier held most of the locals at a respectful distance from the big red wagons and a modest-sized circus tent in the center of about a quarter acre of trampled dusty grass. Longarm could see at a glance how what seemed a combination of a Papist nun and a college don was working the reel brake of the big winch between the wagons to let that balloon rise ever higher, but not too fast for its safe return.

Another oddly dressed figure stood nearby with a cluster of six or eight townsmen dressed a mite more imposingly than some. As Dad Jergens strode over with Longarm in tow he called out, ''I told you not to blow up no more charges with nightfall coming on, ladies! They'll have heard that first one for miles in ever' direction and do those Anabaptists ride, like they said they might, I don't want 'em riding after dark!''

A big portly cuss with muttonchop whiskers got between Jergens and the rainmakers to thunder, ''Leave 'em be and let the National Grange worry about those sun-worshipping Anabaptists! Your mayor and board of aldermen are with the Grange on this. For if we don't get some rain before the Fourth of July, you'll hear the corn popping in the fields instead of fireworks!''

A less self-impressed older gent who likely had more to do with running the settlement called out, more gently but firmly, ''We told the ladies to try some more higher up, Dad.''

Dad Jergens shrugged and just stood there, cussing under his breath. Up closer, Longarm saw the two female scientists didn't look near as spooky. They both wore black sunbonnets and poplin dusters over ecru summer frocks of shantung, which was nubby wild silk a mite lighter than plain old tan. Despite the breezes as the shadows lengthened, they both wore their dusters wide open down the front, with those ecru bodices cut mighty low. So it seemed safe to say both gals were shapely just this side of pleasingly plump. The one controlling the balloon tether had light brown hair. The slightly older one sort of supervising was darker. A man would have a chore figuring which was the better looking. Longarm didn't find either pretty enough to settle down with. On the other hand, he couldn't see throwing either out of bed just for eating crackers between the sheets.

Dad Jergens introduced Longarm all around as a famous federal lawman. The Ruggles sisters answered to Rowena and Roxanne. Longarm didn't care which was which. The older one must have read his mind, for as her sister paid out more line and everyone else went back to staring up at their fool balloon, she moved closer to ask if he wanted to examine their government patents or look through their scrapbook of clippings and testimonials.

Longarm smiled thinly down at her. ''Selling gold bricks or magic beans to simple folks ain't federal offenses, ma'am. Whether you're in violation of Dan'l Ruggles' government patents or not is between you all and him, in civil court. I can tell you what's in your scrapbook without putting you to that much bother.''

47

The darker sister stared up uncertainly. "Have Rowena and me run into you before, Deputy Long? I feel sure we'd have remembered."

Longarm chuckled wryly and said, "I think you're pretty too. Last time you were an old gray professor, sending up clouds of sulfur smoke. Before that you were this goofy-looking young jasper with a swamping kite all studded with tacks. I reckon the grandaddy of you all was this slick cave-man with a drum."

She gasped. "How dare you compare the science of pluvi-culture with superstitious rainmaking rites! I can show you clipping after clipping attesting to our success in other parts, and written by impartial local reporters who never thought we'd do it either!"

Longarm glanced thoughtfully up at the now-tiny golden dot in a purple sky as he quietly replied, "I'll bet you a hundred dollars it ain't going to rain tonight."

To which she replied with an angry face, "My sister and I are not gamblers! We're scientific pluvicultuists and we don't ask anyone to risk a dime on our experiments. Feel free to ask anyone in this crowd if they've been asked to pay in advance for the rain they so desperately need!"

Longarm didn't. He said, "I told you I've met you before, ma'am. You've gotten the Grange, the G.A.R., or mayhaps the First Methodists to ask everyone to chip in, at no risk to themselves if the conditions don't work out right. If you ladies fail to make it rain, everyone gets their money back and you move on friendly with no posse dogging your trail. On the rare occasions it *does* rain, after you've expended a few dollars' worth of dynamite, you collect all that money held in escrow for you and . . . What's the going rate for a good crop-saving rain these days? Four figures? Five? That gent with the sulfur smoke walked away with close to twenty grand one lucky day."

He thought she was going to spit at him. She looked as if she wanted to. Then she smiled sweetly up at him and said she had no idea on earth what he was talking about.

He didn't explain further. She knew. That old boy in that cave with that drum had known better than to ask for a side of mastodon in advance when he offered to stay home and pray for good hunting. Just as he'd known that when and if the others *had* good hunting, they'd be proud to give him a generous share of meat and more credit than he might deserve.

Longarm stayed put as the one called Roxanne flounced over to her sister and murmured something. Longarm figured she was saying that the balloon was high enough. Then, as expected, the younger one set the winch's spool and brought out a blaster's generator box.

It was standard gear you could pick up anywhere they sold dynamite and other blasting supplies. The compact wooden box was lined with permanent bar magnets. There was another one stuck to the moveable plunger. When you shoved the plunger down to move one magnet past a mess of others fast, you got a sudden jolt of twelve-volt current, which was enough to make a swell electric spark most anywhere you wanted to string the attached wires.

Roxanne called out with a voice of authority, "Attention, everyone, fire in the sky!"

Then, sure enough, her sister shoved down hard and the dynamite blew up, a quarter mile above their upturned faces. It made a brighter flash against the darkening sky this time, but the noise was much less impressive and, as far as Longarm could tell, without any other result. So he wasn't surprised when Roxanne allowed they'd try some more later.

He gazed about for Dad Jergens as the crowd began to break up. He wasn't interested in any of this rainmaking nonsense. He wanted the local lawman to explain about more serious stuff. But it seemed tough to keep the old scatterbrain on one topic long enough to matter.

"Screw 'em all but six!" Longarm muttered to nobody in particular as he drifted back towards town with the others. He figured it might make more sense if he just settled up at that corral, gathered his personal stuff, and hired a room somewhere before he tried some saloon gossip. It surely sounded like less trouble, and he doubted the town law here in Cedar Bend would know any more about events in Sappa Crossing than your average nosy local in any case.

By the time he'd made it to the stable next to the corral it was getting darker. Prairie sunsets could be like that when there were no clouds up yonder. He saw Osage Olive had an oil lamp going inside already as he approached the open doorway. She'd doubtless been looking outside to take in the sundown hustle and bustle. For she came to the doorway to greet him. She looked a lot less mannish in the red smock and sash she'd changed to. Those bib overalls had been hiding a shapely pair of ankles above her beaded moccasins.

He hadn't noticed either his hired bay or the paint out in the open corral next door. When he said so the gal replied, "I put 'em inside with fodder and water after a rubdown. Your saddles and harness are in the tack room. Have you eaten yet?"

He shook his head and replied, "I was just about to ask if you knew a good place for a stranger to get some hash around here."

She said, "I can't offer you any hash. But if you'd like to try some roast beef with grits and gravy you've come to the right place. I was just about to have some when they set off all that dynamite out yonder and a bunch of old boys came by to take their ponies on home to their own suppers."

Longarm started to say he didn't want to put her to any trouble. Then he wondered why anyone would want to say a dumb thing like that. Next to a barber, hardly anybody heard more small-town gossip than a hostler helping riders from all about, drunk or sober, get off and on their ponies. So he said he'd be proud to sup with her, as long as he got to pay extra for it.

She said they'd work something out, and led the way back through a tack room, some storage bins, and a narrow hallway into a more brightly lit and sweeter-smelling kitchen. As she seated him at a pine table, she nodded at a curtained doorway across from the small cast-iron range and said that it led to her sleeping quarters.

He hadn't asked. So he wondered why she'd felt the call to tell a male supper guest.

He didn't ask how come she'd cooked enough for two as she dished out generous helpings. She wasn't chubby by white standards. She was downright skinny by those of her own nation. Like most Horse Indians, Osage men prided themselves on providing all the solid grub a wife or more could possibly eat. So a *weya* over twenty-five or so was often a well-fed butterball.

It would have been rude to ask the lady how old she was, or what she did to stay in such fine shape. So he never did. But as they ate and jawed across the table from one another, he found himself learning a tad more about Olive Red-Dog.

She said she'd taken her Indian name back after some Wasichu kin of a late husband had laughed at the notion of any Widow Swenson being so brunette. The Red-Dog family of the Osage Nation were as respected across the Kansas prairie as any towheaded immigrants, as she put it.

When Longarm soberly assured her he'd heard tell of the good fights the Osage had fought for the Union against Confederates, Wasichu or Cherokee, she seemed less defensive, and allowed her poor Gonar had been good to her and taught her a lot before he'd come down with a winter ague and died on her a good two years back. She said he'd had the idea to open a livery along the trail between McCook and Dodge. She said she'd been the one the township council approached to add on a municipal corral as well. They gave her a property tax break in return for her boarding stock that belonged to the town law, the aldermen, and all.

He didn't care. As he let her pour him a second cup of coffee, made Wasichu style instead of with white flour added, he tried to switch the conversation to what Dad Jergens had said about trouble in nearby parts.

Olive didn't know anything about Horst Heger or, naturally, Wolf Ritter. But she could have written a textbook on northwest Kansas. To begin with she'd been born on this same rolling prairie, though a good three hundred miles to the southeast, before the town of Coffeyville had been there and when the buffalo still roamed. So despite being on the softer side of forty, the good old gal had watched Kansas turn white, through good times and bad. She'd been a toddler barely old enough to understand what her elders were talking about when old John Brown had massacred those slaveocrats on the banks of the Pottawatamie. Her nation hadn't thought much of the ''Peculiar Institution'' either.

White folks moving west had met with the friendly buffalo-hunting, tipi-dwelling Osage. So they'd never gotten as famous as their Sioux-Hokan-speaking Lakota or Santee cousins.

Like the Absaroka, Caddo, Ojibway-Crow, Pawnee, and such, the Osage had been sensible enough to change with the times and avoid such destructive habits as shooting up the Seventh Cav, though they'd shown themselves to be ferocious enough against Confederate or Cherokee columns during the war. So Olive, as she had been baptized as a Christian Osage maiden, had married up with the late Gonar Swenson and moved out this way with him while it was still pure cattle country, to watch it fill out a mite as homesteaders of various persuasions edged ever further into dried short-grass prairie.

She told Longarm a bit more about that argument about the weather old Dad Jergens was worried about. She thought it was dumb. Everyone knew it took six medicine men around one big drum, beating it as they chanted in unison, to make it rain.

Like most Horse Indians, as well as the stock raisers who still grazed the higher and drier country all around, Olive was content to let it rain or shine within reason. A rainy day could be a bother. On the other hand, it freshened the short grass and left prairie pools for the stock, saving them longer walks to their regular watering places. You got fatter meat off buffalo, or cows, who hadn't worked too hard at growing up.

Longarm already knew why nesters who plowed and planted late in an uncertain greenup wanted more summer rain than you usually got out in short-grass country. He suspected it made more sense to drill in some of that winter wheat in autumn and roll with the punches. But nobody had asked him for agricultural advice, and Dad Jergens had started to tell him about bank robberies and kidnappings before he'd gotten so distracted.

Olive said Dad did that a lot, and added, "They didn't exacly *rob* the Granger's Trust over in the county seat. They crept in after-hours to crack the safe. The sheriff told the newspaper reporters the crooks had likely been professionals, who'd used nitrate fertilizer."

Longarm gently murmured, "I think you mean nitroglycerine. It's a lot like lamp oil, only it blows up like dynamite because dynamite is only a mixture of nitroglycerine and clay. Safecrackers pour the sort of dangerous juice along the door cracks of a safe, take a deep breath, and smack the whole shebang with a sledgehammer."

The Osage gal poured more coffee for them both as she said, "I see why they call it cracking a safe. How come anyone would want to mix such dangerous juice with clay, Custis?"

Longarm explained, "To make it less dangerous. Liquid nitro can go off in your hands if you stare at it too hard. So nobody had near as much use for it before that Swedish chemist, Nobel, got to fooling with it. He tried mixing it with gunpowder and came close to killing his fool self."

Longarm sipped some of her strong black coffee as he considered a probably dumb notion, dropped it, and continued. "He finally settled on clay, wood flour, or whatever to make paper-wrapped sticks of diluted nitroglycerine that wouldn't swish and blow up when you handled 'em. By the way, what old country did you say your late husband hailed from?"

Olive stared back at him in confusion as she thought, then told him, "Gonar was born in a place called Iceland before his elders brought him to York State as a baby. What's that have to do with high explosives?"

Longarm said, "Probably nothing. What might Dad Jergens have meant when he mentioned kidnappings?"

Olive frowned thoughtfully—Longarm found thoughtful gals sort of pretty—and told him, "We don't talk as much to those Mennonite nesters a fair ride to the south. But I have heard gossip about a wife either running off on her husband or worse. They seemed to be getting along and nobody had noticed her flirting with another man."

He didn't press the Cedar Bend gal for details most anyone in Sappa Crossing would know better. He put down his empty cup and said, "You sure brew fine coffee, Miss Olive. But now we'd best settle on what I owe you so's I can be on my way. For it's dark out now, and I still don't know where I mean to spend the night my ownself."

She glanced over at the one oil lamp in the kitchen, as if deciding whether to turn the wick brighter or dimmer, as she quietly asked him, "Why don't you stay here? Are you too proud, Wasichu Wastey?"

He blinked in surprise and replied, "Your folks never hung such a friendly name on me for acting snooty. I reckon it would make sense for me to unroll my bedding up in your hayloft and get an early start in the morning, if that's what you had in mind, ma'am."

Olive Red-Dog stared pointedly at the curtained doorway leading to her sleeping quarters as she quietly said that hadn't been exactly what she'd had in mind.

So Longarm got to his feet and as the far smaller Indian gal rose expectantly, he just swept her off her moccasined feet and headed out of the kitchen with her as she clung to him and murmured what sounded like *"Oh hinh, iyopte!"* which might have meant she was anxious to get going. *He'd* been

54

wanting to since he'd first seen her ankles in the doorway a hundred hard-up years ago.

But even as he groped their way to her iron bedstead in the dim light of her small clean-smelling sleeping quarters, Long-arm felt he owed it to the gal to say, "You do understand I'll be moving on at sunrise, don't you, pretty lady?"

She replied softly, "I'd never have invited you in here for the night if I thought you might be here long enough to need a haircut. I hate the way you men brag in barbershops, as if you had anything to say about this sort of thing!"

So he laughed like hell and lowered her to the bedding. But then, as he flopped down beside her and reached for a friendly feel, the apparently rough and ready old gal sobbed, "No! Kiss me first. Treat me like a Wasichu girl who means something to you, before you get up and ride on, you brute."

He said he'd get up right then and there if she thought he was being brutal to her.

But she pulled him down against her and felt friendly as hell as she confided she liked it sort of brutal once she warmed up.

Chapter 7

It felt like he was waking up in a thunderstorm. But as Longarm gathered his wits together, he saw that frisky Osage gal had started up again on top, and the way she was bouncing the bed with her brown shapely torso accounted for the way the dawn light through the one little window behind her flickered. The bedsprings creaking under them and the way she kept licking his face like a pup, Indian style, accounted for the impression of rain. He was thrusting his now fully aroused organ-grinder up to meet her downward bouncings when the air outside was rent by another definite roll of thunder.

He didn't care. He rolled her on her back and hooked a bare elbow under each of her tawny knees to spread her wider and enjoy her deeper as she panted and gasped, *"Heya oh toe kaw hey!* I am starting to come again!"

That made two of them, and since she'd assured him more than once by then that she admired a man who could let himself go crazy in her, Longarm enjoyed a long thoroughly selfish climax in her quivering wet innards. As she milked the last drops from him with her astoundingly strong vaginal muscles and crooned, *"Pee-la me-yeah!"* he kissed her collarbone and replied, "Well, thanks your ownself, you hot-as-hell thing. Is it really raining outside this morning?''

Olive said, ''It's dry as a bone. Those Wasichu witko are setting off sky bombs again. But don't leave yet. I know I promised, before we went to sleep, I wouldn't cry when this time came. But now that it has, I want you to make me come again before you go.''

He said he was running low on ammunition, but figured he could fire another salvo dog-style. So she coyly rolled on her hands and knees to let him stand behind her with his bare feet on the braided rug as he admired a broad view of her he'd never had before. He could tell she rode astride a lot. Nothing else pounded a gal's rump to be so firm and sort of mature-looking below such a slender waistline. As she winked her rectal muscles up at him, she giggled and confessed she'd always envied a mare being served by a stud up until now. He'd wondered how she'd learned to arch her spine and pucker like that.

She allowed he'd been taking lessons from horny critters as well by the time they'd managed a protracted mutual orgasm in such an unromantic but practical position.

Then she served him breakfast in bed to show she wasn't sore when he allowed he had no hard feelings for her. It sure beat all how a widow woman who made love so rough and ready could scramble eggs so delicately. He sensed her ulterior motives in treating him to such a swell breakfast when she got back in bed as he was enjoying his second cup of coffee, knelt between his bare ankles and the foot of the bed, and went down on him with her lucious wet lips.

So it turned out he might be able to lay her one more time, as she entreated, after all. But he sure felt stiff, and had a time walking right when they finally got around to saddling up those ponies so a lawman could carry out his damned duties with the sun now scandalously high.

He didn't look back as he rode out. Olive had asked him not to. So there was no saying whether she was waving at him, just standing there, or playing with herself, as she'd threatened she might.

That orange balloon was more like a black dot against the sunrise now, as it slowly rose with yet another charge into what sure seemed a cloudless sky that would have done the Mojave or Sonora deserts proud. As he rode south past the last yard fences, he decided the two sisters had to be new at flimflammery.

The flint cornstalks to either side as he rode between fenced-in forties were still green, but wilted. He spied a sunflower windmill spinning further up the wagon trace. Curious in spite of Billy Vail's orders, he swung the paint he was riding that morning off to where he could peer over a fence into chocolate-colored streaks between the dustier corn rows. They had the crops under groundwater irrigation this close to the creek bed a few furlongs back. But that one windmill, in such cranky winds as they were getting in early high summer, was barely keeping that hardy flint corn alive. Nobody had ever gotten rich on skinny stock or half-parched cash crops. Barley or rye still had half a chance. But that corn needed rain and a heap of it pronto. A light sprinkle that'd leave the ground firm enough for mule-drawn reapers and steam-powered threshers just wasn't going to revive the local corn crop, not if a halfways irrigated field already looked so desperate!

The higher country between mapped water courses was cut up by a confusion of shallower, drier, nameless draws and washes, as a nation calling itself Tsitsissah had taught strangers who called it Cheyenne in a serious of nameless but bitter little skirmishes in these same parts a few short summers back. So Longarm was down in a draw, out of sight of town and vice versa, when the Ruggles sisters set off another blast high in a cloudless sky.

"Greenhorns," he repeated, reining in to light a morning smoke as he considered other quacks he'd met up with in his travels. Even Hopi rain chanters knew enough to wait until rain seemed *possible* before they offered to try. West of longitude 100° you got enough overcast days, or even weeks, with nothing falling from those damned stubborn clouds. But at least rain was *possible* when you saw *some* sky water up yonder. There was nothing you could do in or about a clear, dry sunny sky but wait for some damned clouds. He wondered idly if those self-styled pluviculturists really believed in their patented method of making noise.

There was no telegraph office in either Cedar Bend or Sappa Crossing. He'd asked. The Grange had been drumming for a rail spur or at least more modern communications north of the Smokey Hill River without much luck so far. But wait, if Horst Heger had sent that wire from the county seat twenty miles east of Sappa Crossing . . .

"Forget it!" Longarm warned himself aloud. Nobody'd asked him to investigate buxom rainmakers who might or might not be kin to the real Dan'l Ruggles and might or might not believe in what they were up to with all that noise in a cloudless sky. He'd meant it when he'd told that one sister he didn't have jurisdiction over pesky threats to the local economy. It was a good thing too. For how would it look if a federal deputy showed up every time a Gypsy dealt out tarot cards or Miss Margaret Fox held another spirit-rapping seance by cracking a double-jointed toe under the table? Folk were supposed to know better than to pay good money for harmless pranks. Lawmen had enough to keep them busy chasing the *dangerous* crooks.

Somewhere out ahead hid a really dangerous furriner, trained to kill by one of the best military machines in the business of killing folks. It didn't matter whether Ritter still had that monstrous LeMat or not. The rascal's bloodstained records allowed he could kill with any sort of gun, a cavalry saber, a bowie knife, or in a pinch, his bare hands.

So Longarm rode on, and when those loco sisters set off yet another sky bomb less than an hour later, he didn't even glance behind him. Old Dad Jergens had said they'd likely hear those blasts clean across the prairie in Sappa Crossing. It was their misfortune and none of his own, as long as nobody got in his damned way.

Chapter 8

The ride would have been no more than a dozen miles on a crow. But following a wagon trace across constantly rolling prairie made for a longer row to hoe. So when they topped a rise and Longarm spotted a new-looking windmill, spinning merrily off to the west with blades winking back at the morning sun, he knew somebody had a cattle spread or homestead up here on the higher range.

When he spotted a black Cherokee cow with a calf to match, he had a better grasp on that distant pumping machine. Cherokee beef was bred from Texas longhorn and chunky black beef cows from back East, adding up to a critter that could manage to survive on marginal range without butchering out so dry and stringy. The original longhorn the Western beef industry was based on had never been bred for meat on the table. The North African Moors who'd introduced the hardy breed to Spain ate lamb or mutton when they could get any, while everyone knew Spaniards and Mexicans cottoned to pigs and chickens or even goats for eating. So the longhorns down Mexico way had been intended for hides and tallow. Spanish-speaking folks used leather a lot more than most, while their night-owl habits in a sunny climate called for a whole lot of tallow candles.

As he spied more bred-up beef in the draw beyond, Long-arm knew why their owner was going to that much trouble. During the long depression of the early '70s the folks back East had been as glad to eat any sort of beef as the poor folks of Spain who got the leavings of the bullring. But now that things had picked up under President Hayes and good old Lemonade Lucy, housewives who'd been lucky to serve corned beef and cabbage once a week were demanding filet mignon, or marbled steaks leastways, and turning up their noses at range beef.

He came upon more black longhorns wallowing hock-deep in what a greenhorn might take for wild rye. But Longarm had seen Mex stockmen play that same slick trick. They'd learned it from some of those old-time Moors before they'd chased them back to North Africa.

He'd read somewhere that the desert goatherds of that big Sahara still sowed quick-sprouting seed in those draws they called something like *waddies* in their own lingo. Most of the time nothing happened, or at best the birds got a free meal out of you. But every now and then your undrilled and labor-free seed set root, and the next time you came by with your stock it was *their* turn to feast. Longarm was still working on why anyone ought to cast *bread* on *water*. But risking a sack of oats or rye you could sow without getting down from your saddle made good sense. He made it close to two dozen critters out there in all that rye getting fatter by the minute.

A distant sky rumble seemed to give the grazing cows pause. More than one gazed his way as if he'd done it. He chuckled and quietly said, "Don't look at me, ladies. I think it's silly too."

He topped another rise to gaze at a bigger and neater version of the trail town and surrounding farms he'd just left. Fields of wind-shimmered golden grain stretched clean to the skyline behind the bigger whitewashed structures of what had to be the Mennonite community of Sappa Crossing. But the way ahead seemed to be a matter of some dispute.

The critter had to be a Cherokee steer. No stockman kept more than one or two bulls if he wanted his cows to get any peace and quiet to fatten on. But sometimes the cutting went a mite awry as the spring roundup crew was turning bull calves to steers, and they called such results queer-steers. Impotent geldings, with enough meat left in their loins to behave like horny bulls who couldn't get it up.

Longarm could sympathize with such a critter, even when he hadn't just been used and abused by a horny Osage widow. But he didn't think much of the way the queer-steer was pawing up dust as it held its horns low and its tail high. So he calmly hauled his Winchester from its saddle boot and levered a round in the chamber as he softly suggested, "Don't you do it, Cherokee. I'd play tag with you if I had only one mount to worry about. No way I'm fixing to fool around with two to manage as you charge. So don't charge."

He'd naturally reined in to show he wasn't disputing the right of way just yet. But the queer-steer had its tail up stiff as a poker now, and as it gathered all four hooves together, cocked its head to aim, and lowered it again to get going, Longarm muttered, "Aw, shit," and fired. It was much easier to stop half a ton of madness on the hoof before it could really get moving.

He knew he'd done right when the critter exploded into an all-out rip-snorting charge despite two hundred grains of .44-40 aimed where all the other members of its species were supposed to have their hearts.

As his pony spooked under him, Longarm fired again and gasped, "I reckon you're right, paint. Anywhere you say!"

So he let go of the lead line, and the two hired ponies took full advantage of his invitation to get the hell off the beaten path as that shot-up queer-steer charged down it like a railroad locomotive on hooves!

It collapsed a furlong on in a cloud of dust, of course. By the time Longarm had chased down the bay and retrieved the lead line, the critter who'd been out to gore the three of them had snorted its last and just lay there, not quite useless yet, damn its valuable hide.

He read the dead critter's brand as he cussed it, and saw it went with those friendlier black Cherokee they'd just passed. Then he said, "Well, Lazy B, I sure hope the same folks who owned you own that windmill off to the west. For this day ain't getting any shorter and they never sent me all this way to discuss the price of beef!"

As he headed for those winking blades, he knew he had to track down the queer-steer's lawful owner and settle up. For shooting stock and leaving it to rot was as bad as stealing it, and there was nothing much lower than a cow thief.

Somebody from that more distant spread must have thought so too. For a trio of riders was coming to meet him as he beelined toward that one visible sign of their outfit. They reined in on a rise in a thoughtful manner, likely discussing his unexpectedly honest approach. He'd naturally put his Winchester back in its boot by this time.

As he neared them he saw the one in the middle was a gal, wearing a big white Stetson but seated sidesaddle on her white pony. The two men with her looked more like regular hands. One rode a buckskin and the other a cordovan with white stockings and blaze. All three of them were holding Winchesters across their saddles.

As he got within easy shouting distance, Longarm called out, "I'd be Deputy U.S. Marshal Custis Long and I just now shot a queer-steer branded Lazy B. Might it have been the property of anyone you all might know?"

The gal, somewhat softer-looking up close, called back in a hard enough tone, "That would have been Old Reb. We've been trying to catch him through three roundups now. We know what he was and why you done it. But you'd still best come with us and see what my *athair* has to say about all this."

He said he had to get on to Sappa Crossing. She said it would still there after he'd had some coffee and cake—or a

66

running gunfight, should he make that choice. So he allowed coffee and cake sounded swell.

He doubted she'd really meant it as mean as it had sounded. The imperious snip was old enough to know you didn't gun a federal lawman over a cow. But she was young enough, and pretty enough, to act a tad spoiled. The two hands riding with her shot sidelong glances at her, as if they were trained poodles anxious to please a stern mistress. As they all crested another wave in the sea of grass to spy rooftops and twin silos ahead, he tried once again to ask her what she figured her dead steer had been worth. She told him her *athair* would likely reward *him* for getting Old Reb before he killed someone on the wagon trace and got them sued. Then she repeated it was up to her *athair* and that Himself wouldn't like it if a stranger snubbed their genuine Arbuckle Brand coffee and the finest pastry west of Saint Lou. She said her *athair* had taught their Chinese cook to bake cakes like Granny used to make, at the peril of his heathen life.

Longarm asked how much of range all about they owned fee simple. The stockman's daughter shrugged and said, "We graze what our cows can eat. I think *Athair* filed a government homestead claim on the homespread you see up ahead. After that we just let our thousand head or so graze the open range the buffalo and Mister Lo left fallow for us."

He asked about the farming homesteaders north or south. One of her hands snorted, "That'll be the day some clodhopper busts one acre of Lazy B sod!"

Then he looked away and swallowed hard as the gal in the white hat shot him a look Longarm couldn't read. So he waited and, sure enough, the gal said innocently, "We only range this strip betwixt those corn and wheat growers. Say four miles wide by a dozen miles long, or twice the size of that island they've built New York City on top of. Even farm folks can see how dumb it would be to drill in crops this high and dry. So we never have any trouble with anyone."

One of her hands suddenly found something in the opposite

direction worth a chuckle. So she demurely added, "No trouble worth mention, at any rate. When strangers start driving claim stakes within two miles, then Himself usually invites 'em to supper and, over after-dinner malt liquor, explains the land claims allowed under Brehonic Law."

Longarm had to think hard, and it was a good thing he took books on most everything home from the Denver Public Library, because up until then he'd never had much occasion to even *say* Brehonic Law.

When he did, he said, "No offense, ma'am, but if you'd be citing the ancient Celtic code of Ireland, Scotland, or Wales, American jurisprudence is based on Anglo-Norman Common Law."

She said, "Everybody knows about that mistake. That's why the laws made in Washington make so much trouble out our way. *Athair* says that in the good old days of Brian Boru and that warrior queen of the Picts, Banrigh Sgatha, there was no need to write down deeds or land titles. Land belonged to Himself who first drew water and burned wood on the spread."

He asked if her daddy might be Scotch or Irish.

She said, "Neither. I'd be Iona MacSorley and my people hail from the Hebrides, where the Donald ruled as a king in his own right until the time of Columbus, when such things mattered less. My *sheanairean* were forced to leave their misty isles many years ago. But none of us have forsaken the old ways."

He believed her. He'd met up with her kind before, and knew she'd been taught to speak English without the usual brogue because, where *her* folks hailed from, English was a whole new lingo that had to be learned entirely. He wasn't up to arguing squatter's rights under either Celtic or Anglo-Norman rules with a spoiled beauty. He knew a whole lot of feuding and fussing had resulted in the outlying parts of the British Isles as men of good faith on either side had tried to sort it out fairly. Different notions of right and wrong caused enough trouble this far west.

He couldn't resist asking innocently whether her dear old daddy had noticed any Indians drawing water or lighting dried buffalo chips a few short seasons back.

She had no sense of humor, or no conscience about such matters. She replied without hesitation, "Clan lands are claimed by first use and held by right of the sword. You can look it up."

He smiled thinly and quietly replied, "I don't read Gaelic, but don't you mean held up by the gun, Miss Iona?"

She shrugged and asked if anyone had pressed federal charges in regard to gunplay or the threat of the same.

He allowed her that point, and concentrated on controlling his two ponies as a yellow cur dog met them in the dooryard to snarl and snap as if he meant it. Iona MacSorley yelled at the mutt but it paid her no mind, driven to distraction by the totally strange stock invading its territory. So the sweet-faced gal simply swung her Winchester and shot it, just like that, without even sighting along the barrel.

It took Longarm longer to get his spooked mount back down from the sky. Once he had, she sweetly apologized for not warning him. She added he should have expected it, seeing the way that *cu cuma* had defied a kind mistress.

As they rode wide of the dead dog bleeding in the dust, the front door of the main house they were approaching popped open and a gnomish figure with a white beard and fright wig popped out on the veranda to say something mighty scary in Hebredian Gaelic.

Iona replied in her imperious English, "Bleidir was about to bite into the *boghan* of this quest's mount, *Athair*. He's come to tell you he shot that *tarbh tosgach* the boys called Reb."

The gnome laughed and grinned up at Longarm to say, "*Ceud failte agus toirlinn!* That poorly cut bull was a devil, and have you eaten your fill this day?"

Longarm allowed he'd barely recovered from breakfast, leaving out the naughty parts, as he dismounted and let their hands take charge of his horseflesh. As he followed the gnome and his daughter inside he saw she was tiny and darker, now that she was on her feet with her hat hanging down her spine on its chin-cord. A redheaded Scotch gal he'd met a spell back had explained how nobody knew where those pockets of small dark elfin folks had come from before recorded history. She'd warned him never to ask any such folks if they were kin to that dark mysterious half-sister of King Arthur, Miss Morgana the Fairy.

The two little people sat him down before a baronial 'dobe fireplace with a big round leather shield and some handsome cutlery over the timber mantel. Then Iona went to fetch some refreshments, and her father made him repeat his adventure with their queer-steer. Longarm couldn't resist asking why they hadn't shot old Reb themselves.

The older man's English sounded plain enough. He had more music to his voice than his more Americanized daughter, but neither sounded at all like those vaudeville Scots who said things like, "Tis a bragh bricht moonlit nicht tonicht!" and insisted that was Scotch-English.

None of the old-timers he'd met in these parts, save for good old Opal Red-Dog, seemed inclined to make much sense. They all acted as if they had something, or somebody, more important on their minds. Longarm wasn't of a mind to discuss the price of beef with the owner of the rogue he'd shot. So he asked if it was all right to smoke, and old MacSorley said he'd be proud to have one. So in the end the shooting of that queer-steer ran Longarm two and a half cents as they both lit up his brand.

They'd barely done so when there came a distant rumble, as of thunder, in the clear morning sky.

Old MacSorley said, "*Och, mo mala,* I wish they wouldn't do that. It upsets my *crodh* and if each loses no more than a pound as it runs about, such losses add up!"

Longarm said he didn't think much of dynamiting clear skies in the hopes of rain either. When he got no argument about that, he casually asked how MacSorley and his fellow beef growers felt about a wetter summer than usual, aside from the noise.

The older stockman shrugged and said, "*Is coma leam,* and I doubt the other stockmen care that much either, as long as the trails are dry and the crossings low by the fall roundup. We're on ground too high to worry about flooding, and a wet or dry summer evens out for our *crodh.* Why do you ask?"

Longarm said, "They pay me to ask nosey questions, sir. I agree with you on that rainmaking operation over to Cedar Bend. But I was told some old boys fixing to harvest their winter wheat any minute have made threats against those Ruggles gals."

The crusty old Hebredian snorted, "Och, that'll be the day when an Anabaptist *sgagair* gathers the *comas* to raise his hand against a full-grown woman!"

Iona, coming back into the room with a loaded tray, trilled out, "He means they're gutless sissies, Custis. Which girls do you want beat up, those silly sisters or the runaway wife who's driven our only good gunsmith to distraction?"

As she put the tray of cake and coffee down on a nearby rosewood table, Longarm blinked uncertainly and decided to risk it. "Might we be talking about a Sappa Crossing gunsmith named Heger, Miss Iona?"

She swung her small shapely derriere around to perch it on a low leather hassock as she calmly replied, "Horst Heger is the only gunsmith in Sappa Crossing and the only good gunsmith this side of the county seat. Do you take canned cow and sugar, Custis?"

He said he preferred his coffee black, and as she served them she elaborated. "I should say he *was* the best gunsmith in these parts. I don't know when I'll ever get back a fowling piece I left with him a good two weeks ago. I'm not the only one who's noticed how distracted he's been acting since his

71

child bride ran off on him with some saddle tramp a month or more ago."

Longarm silently sipped some black coffee. She'd been truthful as to the brand. It was almost impossible to brew a bad cup of Arbuckle, which was why it was so popular in cow camps. But it tasted even better poured by a dainty hand from a coffeepot. He had some of their fine marble cake as well before he decided the risk of asking these outsiders outweighed asking Horst Heger's High Dutch neighbors, or the distraught gunsmith himself. So he asked Iona MacSorley what else they'd heard about the small-town scandal out here a half-hour from town.

She said she'd never had much truck with Heger's missing wife, save to notice she seemed shy and sort of pretty in a dishwater-blond way. The Scotch-American gal explained, "She didn't speak much English. Or at least she never had anything to say to *me* in any lingo. Since my only truck with those Mennonites is purely business, I can't give you any exact dates. I never *asked* my gunsmith where his fool wife might be when I didn't see her peeking through the door in the back at us. I was over to the ladies' notions shop, picking up sewing supplies, when I overheard an English-speaking nester woman complaining about her man being low on birdshot shells because that fool of a Dutchman had forgotten to send for them."

Iona cut another slice of cake for Longarm, without waiting for him to finish the first, as she went on. "I spoke up about the fowling piece he never seemed to get around to fixing, and that was when the Mennonite shopkeeping lady told us we had to be patient with the poor man because his woman had strayed. That's what religious folk's call a wife running off with another man, straying."

It was her gnomish father who quietly asked why a lawman from out Denver way gave toad squat, or something that sounded as bad in the Gaelic, about the domestic tranquility of a local gunsmith.

Longarm decided half truth might be the best policy, and tried to sound as bemused as he washed down some cake to gather his thoughts, then told them both, "I'm following up a report on a wanted man who may have passed this way with an unusual side arm. So arm. So my boss suggested I have a word on that with any gunsmiths such a gunslick might have done business with."

It didn't work. Iona had already shown herself more interested in guns than most gals. When she asked what was so unusual about the gun of that wanted man, Longarm thought some more, decided a lie might be riskier than partly revealed truth, and said, "A lethal cap-and-ball antique called a LeMat, Miss Iona. It was invented in France, but heaps of Confederate gunsmiths copied it during the war because it was right popular with their cavalry raiders."

She nodded and said, "Nine .40-caliber rounds in the wheel and a .66-caliber shotgun barrel thrown in for added conviction."

Longarm smiled across the table at her. "You've seen such a horse pistol, Miss Iona?"

She replied, "In Heger's window. On sale. I asked about it and you were right, picking up such ammunition would be a chore. The one Heger has for sale is converted to take brass .40-25 rounds now. I never asked about that shotgun backup. I lost interest as soon as they said I had to send so far for the special pistol rounds."

Longarm was grateful for the chaw of marble cake in his mouth. For by the time he'd rinsed it down he saw there was no call to go into how a small-town gunsmith in remote parts had come by such an unusual gun. Horst Heger would know better than anyone, and it might be just as well if nobody else got to gossiping about it.

He made more small talk about the rising beef prices that year, quietly satisfied himself the Lazy B riders weren't likely to bother either their wheat-growing or corn-growing neighbors in the immediate future, and allowed he'd love to stay but he had to get it on down the road.

Iona MacSorley announced she was riding into town with him. One got the impression she never asked anyone's permission to do anything. Her gnomish father seemed to think it was a grand notion. Longarm had no right to forbid a grown woman the use of a public right-of-way to most anywhere she might want to follow it. So in no time at all she'd turned the coffee tray and crumbs over to the household help, and the two of them were cutting across the short grass at an angle because the gal said it would be shorter and she didn't want to watch anyone skinning out Old Reb in any case. He'd already noticed, mounting up in the dooryard, how that dead dog had sort of evaporated into thin air. You had to sort of keep your eye on things if you expected them to be there the next time you looked.

Chapter 9

The settlement of Sappa Crossing was still about where he'd been expecting it, off to their southeast as they rode over the last of the Lazy B rises. As they angled down the long slope to the nearly dry creek bed, Longarm saw nobody had planted wheat on that sunnier slope facing into the hotter summer winds from the south. But the ever westward trend of the sodbuster was only getting started. So he asked the cow gal riding to his right what her daddy, or *athair*, meant to do when newcomers filed on his side of Sappa Creek, as was inevitable as death and taxes.

The stockman's spoiled child seemed sincerely puzzled by such a question. She said, "They can't. *We* graze all the open range between the Sappa and the south divide of the Cedar."

Longarm nodded but said, "On public land, save for the few acres you hold lawful title to. Right now the land office would rather see longhorns than buffalo and buffalo-eating Indians out this way. But the Homestead Act of '62 was meant to make the West even more taxpaying. So we're only talking a question of time."

She shook her head stubbornly and insisted, "We can't afford to let anyone crowd us closer. *Athair* was very understanding about those corn and barley growers to the north, and as you see, those Anabaptists down yonder know better than to plant winter wheat where you might get a warm sunny day in January. Nobody but a grasshopper-loving fool would claim any more of our natural *duthas*. Anyone can see it's marginal short-grass range above the high-water mark!''

To which Longarm could only morosely reply, ''If fools were not allowed to file homestead claims, you wouldn't see half as many new wire and windmills out this way. There's already been ugliness in other parts where folks following different traditions move on to recently vacated Indian lands. My job would be easier if everyone headed out this way from all over creation agreed the laws of These United States were the only ones that counted.''

She repeated, in a more American way, what her father had taught her about water, fire, swords, and such. It seemed tough to argue a lick of sense into anyone who considered Arapaho-Cheyenne home range a Hebredian *duthas*, to be held against all comers by some sort of half-ass highland clan. Longarm had read enough history books from that library to know how such old boys had made out against Redcoats and cannon under that prissy Prince Charlie just before the way more important French and Indian War on this side of the main ocean. But while he could have told her about all that, he knew she didn't want to be told, so he didn't tell her.

As they were fording the shallow braided creek to the west of the town—you could really cross the Sappa most anywhere—Longarm's mind was naturally on more important matters. So he had to jerk his attention back to the perky little brunette when she suddenly announced she took a bath every Saturday night and rinsed her hair with larkspur lotion once a month whether she'd felt any nits in her hair or not.

Longarm smiled in some confusion, and assured her he hadn't been about to tell a lady she'd struck him as unwashed or lousy.

Iona pouted. ''I don't think you've been thinking about me at all. You've been treating me like a bitty *nighneag* since first we met. I may be small for a woman grown, but I'm womanly enough where such things matter, and why haven't you sparked at me even once?''

Longarm chuckled gently and truthfully replied, ''It never occurred to me, Miss Iona. I don't mean you ain't good enough for me to spark with. It's just that, like I told you before, I have a heap on my mind and you wouldn't want to get my hopes up, seeing I won't be around all that long.''

She blazed, ''You *are* talking to me as if I was a little girl! A woman can tell when a man's not interested in her as a woman, and I can't say I like your attitude, you snooty thing!''

He said he was sure she was used to being sparked at. It would have been dirty, to both ladies concerned, if he'd told her why he doubted he could get it up again with a block and tackle after that last dry effort in that friendly Indian. So he just repeated what he'd already told her about more serious stuff, and she suddenly reined in and sobbed, ''*Och, as an sin thu*! Go on about your airy-fairy business, and I'm off to buy some ribbon bows and mayhaps spark with some real men!''

Longarm had no call to argue as she cut away at a sharper angle, knowing the back ways of the trail town ahead much better. Being a stranger to Sappa Crossing, Longarm perforce rode on up to the main street. Aside from not wanting to get turned around in some blind alley, he didn't want anyone spooking the town law with tales of an armed stranger poking around out back.

As he swung on to that wagon trace where it widened out to become the main street of a dinky trail town, he was mildly surprised, as he'd been the last time, by how natural Mennonites looked.

Unlike some Pennsylvania Dutch sects or even the English-speaking Mormons out Utah way, the Anabaptist farm folks from far-away prairie country seemed to belong out on the American prairies, like the new kinds of wheat and that one big species of tumbleweed they'd introduced from those back steps of Russia.

Even Indians who should have known better seemed to feel those big fat Russian tumbleweeds had always been tumbling around out here, though in fact the biggest native American tumbleweed had now been reduced in rank to "witch grass."

The soberly dressed folks Longarm passed as he rode in could only be distinguished from ordinary Western rustics by straw hats and chin whiskers on most of the men, and perky white half-bonnets on most of the ladies. The signs along the street were in both English and High Dutch. Longarm knew that a sort of big white barn was their meeting house, and he'd been assured nothing as odd as Holy Rolling went on inside. Hardly anyone would have noticed such a natural-acting religious sect if the Mennonites hadn't been changing the country between the Mississippi and the Rockies far more, in their own quiet way, than the Mormons had on the far side of the Continental Divide. Longarm had recently read how, at the rate things were going, there'd be more white Americans of High Dutch or Irish descent than any other breed by the turn of this century.

Of course, most of the immigrants quietly flocking in from all parts of that Dutch-speaking hodgepodge Bismarck and his kaiser had only recently hammered together as the Germanic Empire were Lutheran or even Papists. But whether they were outnumbered or not, it was the Mennonite Dutch who'd taught everyone else how to make a good living farming what Pike and Fremont had agreed to call the Great American Desert. That Turkish brand of winter wheat the Mennonites had put on the American market wasn't just a grain you could grow on buffalo range. It was a *superior* sort of hard wheat that came out of those big steam-powered mills back East as the finest grade of flour. So when anyone bragged on American apple pie, whether they knew it or not, they were bragging on a Pennsylvania Dutch recipe baked in a crust of Russian-Dutch flour.

A plain American-looking gent with a pewter star pinned to the front of his clean white shirt was regarding Longarm from

78

a doorway with some interest as the dustier federal deputy dismounted in front of the town hall. Longarm had pinned his own badge to the lapel of his old denim jacket as he'd ridden in from the Lazy B with that imperious brunette. He'd found in the past he could save local lawmen harsher words than they could gracefully retract if they knew right off who they might be cussing at. A total stranger of the Anglo-Saxon type wasn't going to ride into a community such as this without anyone of innocent or guilty intent taking note of his arrival. So in this case a frontal attack seemed as safe as any.

That didn't mean a lawman on the trail of another stranger to the close-knit community couldn't zigzag a mite in case Wolf Ritter had made more friends so far than *he* had. So when the Dutch-sounding town marshal said to call him Werner Sattler, they shook on it and Longarm told him the truth halfways as he tethered the two ponies out front. He said he'd heard an owlhoot rider wanted by the federal government had been reported in this corner of Kansas.

The town law nodded soberly and said, "Wolfgang von Ritterhoff. You've missed him by a week."

"You knew who he was, and where he was, and you never saw fit to let the rest of us in on it?" Longarm demanded with a scowl.

The town law replied with what appeared an easy conscience, "He was gone before anyone told me. Come on inside. I don't have any bread and salt in my office desk, but we keep schnaps filed under S."

Longarm followed the town law through that side door of the town hall, and confirmed his memory of schnaps as a strong but smooth brandy to be consumed in moderation while on duty. So he nursed the tumbler Sattler had poured him as they sat on either side of the older lawman's desk to jaw about wayward Prussians with dueling scars.

The town law explained, "That killer trained by the Prussian Army rode in on a market night. So nobody would have paid any attention to him if he hadn't spoken Hoch Deutch."

Longarm started to ask a dumb question. Then he nodded and said, "I follow your drift. A stranger talking English with a Boston accent would attract more attention in a Texas saloon than your average Mex. By the way, you do have saloons here in Sappa Crossing, don't you?"

The Mennonite lawman nodded, raised his glass, and said, "We are good Christians and Our Lord poured wine at the Last Supper. I wish you other Christians would get over the idea we're some sort of cult."

Longarm said, "You won't be as noticeable a generation or so down the road. Your kids are already talking like everyone else out this way. But we were talking about Wolf Ritter, as he's more often named on many a wanted flyer."

Sattler finished his schnaps, poured himself another, and explained, "Our saloon, like some of the other establishments serving the wagon-trace traffic, serves a mostly English-speaking crowd, and as you just pointed out, none of *our* crowd speaks Hoch Deutch in that guttural Junker accent. People from Stettin or Berlin always sound as if they have sore throats."

Longarm was in no position to agree or disagree. So he just took another sip of schnaps and Sattler continued. "There's no law against speaking like a Prussian bully. Fred Zimmermann, at the Ganseblumchen, was the one who brought the mysterious beer drinker to our attention. The bartender's description did match up with a lot of those wanted posters you just mentioned. But by the time I gathered a few of my part-time deputies and got over there, he'd left."

Longarm knew better than to accept another schnaps before he'd had his noon dinner. So he got out two smokes as the older lawman went on. "That LeMat revolver was the persuader. I never saw it in Horst Heger's window until the next morning. So I'd almost put the mysterious drifter out of my mind when someone said they'd seen him riding on. Then, later in the morning, passing Heger's shop, I saw the wicked weapon on sale. I went right inside to ask Heger about it. He said he'd bought it, at a fair price, from a fellow Prussian down on his luck.''

"Horst Heger's as pure Prussian as Wolf Ritter?'' Longarm asked.

The Mennonite shrugged and allowed few Prussians were pure anything, being a mixture of pagan Polish peasants and the Teutonic knights who'd crusaded hell out of 'em back in those Dark Ages.

The local lawman didn't say Horst Heger had recognized Wolf Ritter from those wars of conquest a few summers back. So Longarm figured he'd been smart to play his cards close to the vest. He'd ask Horst Heger when he talked to him.

Once he had his tumbler drained and both their cheroots going good, Longarm casually asked just where Horst Heger's gun shop might be in case that LeMat was still in the window.

The town law said it was upslope, across from the smithy, so a cowhand having his pony reshod might have easy access. On the way back out front, Longarm asked about local liveries, hotels, and such.

The local lawman said there was a municipal corral out back of the town hall. But folks around Sappa Crossing already *had* enough riding stock to make a livery stable unprofitable. When he mentioned they had a fair livery run by a friendly Indian gal just up the ways in Cedar Bend, Longarm changed the subject to wayside inns.

Sattler said they hadn't had one in Sappa Crossing since that mail stage had cut its runs back to once a week, only stopping long enough to matter up in Cedar Bend. He said there was a guest hostel out back of the Mennonite meeting house across the way, and suggested they might put a stranger up for the night.

Longarm said he didn't know how to say grace in High Dutch, and didn't mind sleeping out under the stars in dry weather if he had to. Meanwhile, he had to find out how long he was likely to be in these parts.

Following Sattler's easy directions, Longarm rode the bay

and led the paint the short distance upslope to where, sure enough, he saw a big wooden rifle, painted gold, across from the open front of the smithy, where a bunch of men and boys were watching the blacksmith shoe a monstrous dapple gray drafthorse that just didn't think it needed new shoes.

Longarm passed by the amusing antics and High Dutch cussing to rein in and dismount across the way, tethering his ponies to the hitching rail near a handy water trough. He took his tempting Winchester from his McClellan, and stepped up on the plank walk to see that there really was a LeMat nine-shooter for sale in the front window.

Someone had written in High Dutch and English on a card propped against the trigger guard of the dramatic weapon. Longarm bent lower to read what the English writing said. That was why the bullet aimed at the nape of his neck just took his hat off for him as it flew on to shatter that plate glass all to flying bits!

Longarm had been taught by a war in his teens that the best way to duck for cover was the way someone aiming a second shot might not be expecting. So he dove headfirst through the now glassless front window of the gunsmith's shop to roll through the crepe-paper curtain behind the display and land flat on his ass in a pile of busted glass and scattered shooting irons with some woman screaming fit to bust from the gloom beyond.

He yelled at her to shut up and take cover as he rolled over to rise up on one knee, levering a round into the chamber of his saddle gun as he glared out through all that confusion for something to aim it at.

But the street out front was a milling swirl of men, boys, rising dust, and at least three horses screaming bloody murder as they tried to bust loose. So Longarm rose to his full height and turned to the screaming gal behind him to say, ''It's over for now. I never busted your front window with my fool head, ma'am. Someone was shooting at it, or at me, from across the way. As an educated guess, I'd make it from that dark slot betwixt yonder smithy and the feed store next to to it.''

"Was kann ich fur Sie tun, mein Herr?" didn't sound as if she was following his drift.

He asked for Horst Heger. She brightened and gushed, *"Ich weiss es noch nicht.* I can a little English when you slow speak it. I am Helga Pilger and I haff only here started. Herr Heger has just me hired to watch for him when he somewhere goes.''

Longarm could see why. The big buxom blonde was busting out of the peasant blouse and laced-up bodice above her pleated red calico skirts. It hardly mattered if anything that pretty spoke English in a High Dutch-speaking town, or had the brains of a gnat behind those big blue eyes.

He was still admiring the view when his attention was drawn to the fuss outside, and he turned from the Mennonite maiden to see old Werner Sattler, the town law, climbing through that busted-in shop window to join them, saying, *"Zum Teufel!* I thought they might have had you in mind! The men across the street say the shot was fired from the feed store, but the boy in the feed store thinks it came from the . . . *Schmiede* next door.''

The lawman's English was so much better than Helga's that it came as a surprise to hear him grope for less familiar words. Longarm nodded and replied, "I reckon you mean smithy, and I made it that narrow slot betwixt the two. I'm still working on who might have been so sore at me. Will you look at this mess!''

Sattler said, "Whoever it was won't get far. I've sent deputies out in every direction to cover the outskirts of town, and it's not as if we're surrounded by Das Schwarzwald—I mean the Black Forest.''

Longarm said, "I know what you mean. Anyone crawling through ripe grainfields on hands and knees would leave a trail a schoolmarm could follow, and it's just after high noon outside, so pony dust can be seen. But let me ask you something, no offense. How many folks do you reckon you'd have in town just now, whether resident or just in for some shopping or other fun?''

The town law thought. ''About a hundred and ten families of fellow Mennonites, perhaps a dozen of other faiths, and there might be two dozen individuals off the surrounding spreads at any given time. But not many of them would be strangers to my deputies. We're looking for a stranger. That Wolfgang von Ritterhoff, *nein*?''

Longarm said, ''Nine and a question mark. Sounded like a common old .44-40 round, the most popular caliber for the thinking shootist, and who says it has to be a stranger? That bullet missed me by a whisper, and I got the distinct impression it was aimed my way by someone who knew me on sight from a distance!''

Chapter 10

Longarm got them to stable his stock behind the smithy. He knew he didn't know who belonged in the township. So he stayed behind to help the bewildered Mennonite maiden tidy up. He gingerly picked up and wiped off the scattered guns as Helga swept up the busted glass. As they worked together she drew him a clearer picture of the situation. Her English seemed to get better, or else he got better at figuring out what she was trying to say. Her old country grammar was something like Olde English had started out. When you thought about how English was strung together in King Arthur or the Good Book, you weren't half as confounded by someone saying something like, "I have but two weeks been out with this shop helping."

Her story, in plain English, was that she'd been born on those back steps of Russia, been orphaned up in the Dakotas by that ague going about a few winters back, and sent down here to Kansas by Dakota kin to see if she'd like to marry up with one of the Brethren who'd filed on a hundred and sixty acres and was anxious to file on more in the name of most any wife who'd have him.

Helga had decided she didn't want him. She said one look

85

had been enough to inspire some doubts before he'd asked her to dig postholes while he cooked supper. She said the clincher had been his forgetting to offer her bread and salt when he met her stage in Cedar Bend.

Longarm had to think back. Then he nodded and said, "I'd forgot that Russian habit your kind picked up living under the czars. But anyone can see it's an easy way to make a newcomer feel welcome. He could have just felt it was too old-timey for a brand-new American to bother with, though."

Helga hunkered down to sweep some glass into a copper dust pan as she protested, "In that case he could have flowers, books, or candy met me with. I have courting cowboys watched. A *schnorrer* is still a *schnorrer* no matter how the customs followed are!"

"He snored too?" Longarm asked with a wry grimace.

Helga blanched and protested, "*Schnorrer* in my *zunge* is the same as a bum in your own. I never stayed out at his dusty sod *Hutte* to about him that much learn! I here in town found a job as a *putzenfrau*—I mean cleaning woman—with a *lutherisch* family. My poor mother was so wise to leave me to choose what I would be *after* I had up grown! I am sure I don't *schwesterlich* wish *mein Taufe*. That is in English baptism, *nicht*?"

Longarm regarded the gaping storefront thoughtfully as he replied without a whole lot of interest, "It's a free country, Miss Helga. You can pray to the Great Jehovah or Wakan Tonka for all my department will pester you. Might your boss, Horst Heger, have any lumber handy? You were fixing to tell me more about where he'd gone and when you expected him back before we got sidetracked into bread and salt, remember?"

She said, "There is in the *keller* a workbench and some boards, I think. Herr Heger never told me where he was going or when he was to back return. I have not since last week seen him. I no longer to our old services go. But *naturalich* I did

86

not on *Sonntag* miss him. I opened *Montag Morgen* and have since then been the shop trying to run for him. I know little about guns. But most of our trade is ammunition and supplies.''

He told her to stay topside and watch the store while he went down to the cellar to see about that boarding. He struck a match on the steep wooden steps and found an oil lantern hanging handy on a nail. It still took two genuine wax matches from Old Mexico to get the lamp burning right. The 'dobe-walled and dirt-floored cellar was spiderwebby and stinky for that late in summer. The place needed airing out. When he spied a flight of brick steps leading up to what had to be a sloping exit to the backyard, he made a mental note to mention airing to young Helga.

Meanwhile he gathered up some pine planks apparently salvaged from some other building, found a hammer and a mason jar of mixed nails, and hauled it all upstairs.

As he put his hat and jacket aside to get to work up front, he told Helga about that outside cellar door. She said she knew about it, and had noticed how rank the dirt cellar smelled, but that her boss had the only key to the padlock sealing the stink in.

He told her to open the front and back doors upstairs at least, and left the cellar door open as he hammered together a lattice of odd lengths of lumber in hopes of letting in some air while keeping small boys out. He had to make more than one trip. Seeing Helga seemed more comfortable with him now, he took a mite more time in the cellar and found a whole sheaf of wanted flyers and reward posters in an old chest of drawers across from the workbench. Longarm left them where they were for now. They weren't his, and it stood to reason a gunsmith who'd spotted an owlhoot rider packing an unusual gun had been making a sort of hobby out of collecting wanted papers. A gunsmith too dumb to know outlaws were interested in guns might have never recognized a renegade with a LeMat for sale.

Back upstairs, nailing a diagonal plank with shorter nails than he might have bought from scratch, Longarm told Helga, "That ought to keep casual prowlers out. But all these guns are too valuable to leave out after your regular closing time. Is there some safer place I could help you store them, if you'd like me to come back?"

She said her boss had always put such tempting stock away in a vault in the back. Then she asked where he was going before closing time.

He said he'd know better once he got there, and asked her to show him their vault.

That turned out to be a combination vault, big enough to walk into, if only it had been open. Helga said only her boss had the combination, and she'd been mighty worried about that. She'd found all the stock in the cases out front, just as they'd been when she'd tidied up Saturday noon, when she reported for work the following Monday with her key to the front door. She said she'd felt she'd had no choice but to keep things humming as best she could until her fuzzy-headed but kindly boss got back from wherever on God's green earth he'd gone. Helga insisted on showing Longarm the modest receipts in the till, as if he had any notion how much money was supposed to be there.

He made the mistake of saying that. So the next thing he knew the strapping blonde had dragged him into the back quarters, where Helga had a small kitchen set up, and made him sit at a table with a pile of business ledgers as she puttered about making them a snack.

Longarm leafed through the dry dusty ledgers with about the same interest he'd have shown to the scrapbook of some touring piano player, Everything was printed in High Dutch. But figures were figures, and ink came red or black in any lingo. So almost despite himself, Longarm found himself paying attention to another man's business.

Business had been lousy lately. The profit on ammunition and new supplies was less than fifty percent. Longarm had pals in the trade out Denver way, so he knew there was purer profit in repairing and altering guns. But Mennonite farmers and even the local cowhands had placed damned few orders for tailored gun grips, hair triggers, and such. Longarm noticed other entries showing Heger had taken used guns on consignment, meaning the original owner only got paid if and when his gun was sold. Longarm looked back a few pages, in vain, as Helga dished out generous portions of what looked like kitten's brains mixed with bloody cedar shavings. "There's something I don't savvy here," he said.

She told him they were having *Blaukraut mitt Blumerkohl* and that everyone drank tea from glasses in her old country.

He said that wasn't what he was worried about. He explained, "That LeMat on sale in the window for twenty whole dollars ain't on the books here at any price."

He had to explain which gun was a LeMat before Helga was able to tell him she wasn't sure how long it had been in the window or who'd consigned it to them for sale.

The oddly named grub turned out to be pretty good pickled cauliflower and red cabbage. The Russian-Dutch tea helped a heap with its sort of sour aftertaste. She seemed more puzzled as to why he found a gun in the window of a gunsmith shop such a puzzle.

He said, "Whether your boss took it on consignment or paid cash, it should have been listed in the ledgers. And they were asking way too much. Twenty dollars would buy you a spanking-new Colt '73, and a factory-fresh Remington would run you less."

She suggested perhaps the owner had set the price on the gun over Herr Heger's mild objections. She said with a smile that her boss never seemed to really fuss with anyone.

Longarm washed down some red cabbage and said, "I noticed. Going over his books just now, it's easy to see why he might have been anxious to make some money on the side. When you say he acted sort of fuzzy, did you mean absent-minded fuzzy or drinking fuzzy, Miss Helga?"

She allowed the missing gunsmith could have had either a troubled mind, a drinking problem, or both. She hadn't even known Heger when his wife ran off on him that spring. She said he'd put a sign in the front window saying he could use some help, and hadn't put up too much of a fuss when she'd barged in to say she'd rather keep shop than clean house. As Longarm got her to go over it all again, he saw she really didn't know as much about Horst Heger as *he* did. The missing gunsmith had never confided in his new hired help about wanted outlaws he could turn in for bounty money. He'd been sort of fuzzy about paying her any wages and owed her for two weeks. To Helga's credit, or slow wits, she'd been living on the odds and ends of grub back here in the kitchen without dipping into the till.

Longarm tried to help her out in a graceful way by allowing he was in the market for a couple of dollars' worth of Remington .44-40s and suggesting she had no call to record the sale before her boss came up with her back wages.

But while Helga led him back out front and rustled up the hundred rounds for him, she explained all such sales had to be entered in yet another notebook, although a smaller one, under the till.

He asked to see it as the buxom gal primly put his two cartwheels in the till. He saw at a glance that this extra record only dealt with ammunition. He saw why when he noticed some entries were notations on special orders. Thanks to the many mighty clever or ambitious machinists who'd noticed the original breech-loading or revolver patents had run out in recent years, there was now a whole lot of makes and models on the market, some of them shooting mighty odd ammunition, such as that special caliber for the czar's picky cavalry. Longarm looked for some, and sure enough, found more than one order for that .429-23 made for all those Smith & Wesson six-guns specially ordered by the Grand Duke Alexis while he was hunting buffalo with Bill Cody.

The czar's fool cavalry had never taken delivery on those fool revolvers. So S&W had put them on the American market, cheaper than a matching model that fired regular American brass. You found out after you bought one that you had to send back East, to one factory at three cents a round, to load your bargain side arm.

Longarm guessed, and Helga confirmed, that the Russian S&W was a lot more popular than it should have been in Russian-Dutch Mennonite country. He saw they had more on hand than the average shop of this size would have. But then, try as he might and going back over a month, he failed to find any mention of that queer ammunition you fed a LeMat.

Helga didn't seem to find that meaningful. So he told her, "Tough to sell an unusual gun at a high price without letting anyone peg a few shots out back. Let's see if there's any shells in the thing."

As she followed him along the other side of the counter to where he'd placed the LeMat from the busted-up front display, Helga shook her blond head and insisted, "*Ich glauben nicht*. An idiot only would leave a loaded gun in *das Fenster*!"

But when Longarm examined the massive LeMat more closely, he found the shotgun chamber empty but five live rounds in the nine-shot wheel. He raised the loaded weapon to his mustache and sniffed before he told her, "It ain't been cleaned since someone fired at least three rounds. One chamber was riding empty under the firing pin, but you can see the spent brass in these other three."

91

She gasped, "So *schmutzig*! Any gun will outrust when you clean it not after firing, *ja*?"

Longarm went on emptying the LeMat as he agreed. "That's about the size of it. I doubt anyone ever intended to sell this antique. Twenty dollars was way too high a price to set, Heger had no ammunition for a big spender who *might* have wanted the fool thing, and like you just said, leaving a gun to lay about with a fouled barrel ain't the way you're going to keep it in mint condition!"

He held up the empty LeMat to squint through it at a chink in those front boards, then whistled and marveled, "I wouldn't give five dollars for this poor brute with a hundred rounds of that fancy French ammunition thrown in! As your boss has likely told you already, the sulfur and saltpeter traces left in the grooves after hot spinning lead has wiped away every trace of oil can suck moisture from the air way faster than clean steel just left to rust."

He put the weapon, now less valuable, back on the countertop and mused aloud, mostly to himself, "Try her this way. Ritter's having as much trouble loading a freak gun, he knows it's been mentioned on more than one wanted flyer, so he drops by a trail-town gunsmith to trade it in for something less unusual. Heger recognizes him but naturally never says so. He goes along with the deal, more interested in getting the rascal out of his hair than—"

"*Bitte*, who is this Herr Ritter?" Helga cut in.

Longarm said, "Never mind. If you've ever met him since, he was using another name. Heger must have expected him to be in town for a spell. That's why he put the LeMat in the window. He priced it high so he'd still have it on hand when someone like me showed up."

She said she didn't know what he was talking about. He smiled and assured her she wasn't to worry her pretty little head about it. Then he asked why she was getting all teary-eyed.

92

She said, "I am not so a stupid cow! Maybe I don't so good the English speak, but I can read and write and also add and subtract!"

He said he was sure she was running the shop just fine, and promised to come back later with some sensible groceries before he rode on.

Chapter 11

Longarm collected some odd looks as he strode up to the town hall with his Winchester muzzle aimed politely at the planking. he figured it was likely because of his mustache. He'd noticed most of the homesteading Mennonites wore full beards, Abe Lincoln beards, or shaved their whole face. Mennonite gals must have disliked whiskery kisses as much as Mexican gals admired them. He noticed it was the younger and more likely single locals who shaved and got regular haircuts. At the rate they were going those total furriners would be passing for real Americans in no time, and folks would think names like Taft, Treumann, or Welk had always gone with these parts.

When he got to Werner Sattler's office, a kid deputy told Longarm the town law was still out trying to separate the sheep from the goats. He said they were holding a couple of drifters back in their one patent cell, but doubted either one had pegged a shot at anyone in recent memory.

Longarm said he'd be over at that saloon with the unpronounceable name when and if Sattler wanted him. The kid deputy laughed and said Gansenblumchen just meant Daisy. Longarm was too polite to ask why they had to use such long words for every fool thing.

Once he got there, the Gansenblumchen turned out to be a beer garden as well as a saloon. You drank inside when the sun was blazing down hard at the tables and chairs set up under cottonwoods and paper lanterns out back.

As his eyes adjusted to the sudden shade inside, Longarm saw the taproom was better than half empty. That made sense in mid-afternoon on a working day. He figured the mostly older gents nursing mostly beer were in town with a crop in the fields and a woman interested in some pokey shopping. Many a saloon would have no call to open during business hours if women shopped like men and just got it over with.

As he bellied up to the bar, he took out his pocket watch to check it against the ornate wall clock above the back bar. If they were right he was running a tad slow. When he wore his three-piece suit around the Denver Federal Building, his watch and pocket derringer rode in separate vest pockets on the same gilt chain. Having everything jumbled together in one breast pocket of a charro-length denim jacket couldn't be doing his old timepiece a whole lot of good.

A well-fed barmaid with her auburn hair pulled up into a considerable bun came down his way with an easygoing smile to ask, *"Was willst du, Kuhhirt?"*

Longarm smiled uncertainly and replied, "If you're asking what I want, I'd sure like a stein of beer, ma'am."

She seemed to think that was funny as hell. But she poured him a pint of cool draft as she said she hadn't thought he was from around Sappa Crossing. He didn't say just who he might be or where he might hail from. So as he sipped some suds she decided, "You must be for *der Schottisch Viehzuchter,* Herr MacSorley, riding. Some of our own have also *Kuhhirten,* I mean cowboys, become since the price of beef has so high gone."

Since she'd *told* him what he was supposed to ask, he felt no call to correct her. Sometimes Longarm was surprised by what he could learn just keeping his mouth shut and his ears open.

As she moved to serve an old cuss at the far end things got back to normal for a lazy afternoon in a taproom. Gents who'd stopped talking to see what a stranger might have to say for himself went back to talking among themselves, mostly in High Dutch. Longarm found the lingo sort of infuriating. Some words sounded almost the same as English, but just as you figured you were following the drift, it lit out like a cutting horse in another direction entirely. He'd leafed through a dictionary one time to confirm that while *Hund* meant hound, *Henne* meant hen, and a *Kuh* was a cow, they up and called a rabbit something that sounded like "hoss," and you asked a lady if she'd like to fart when you meant to take her for a buggy ride. A lot of their innocent words sounded sort of dirty. He wondered what dirty words in English sounded like in High Dutch. There was no polite way to ask that barmaid. So he didn't.

Two other gents dresses like *Kuhhirten* or cowboys were having what sounded like a soft but heated argument at a corner table behind him. They were too far away for Longarm to make out any words. But once you'd spent a few hours listening to furriners, it was surprising how Tennessee an old boy could sound when he twanged just loud enough to hear.

Longarm edged along the bar until he had a better view of them in the back-bar mirror. Neither seemed aware of him as they argued softly but seriously. From gestures and expressions alone, Longarm got an impression one was all for moving on, while the older and cooler-looking cuss was for staying right where they were, as if they were waiting for someone.

Longarm was good at faces. But he couldn't match either of the nondescript cowhand types with any serious descriptions on file. So he finished his beer, left some small change on the bar, and sauntered out without looking back.

He moved faster out on the walk. He'd almost made it back to the town hall when two other total strangers seemed anxious to have a word with him.

The taller of the two said, "If you'd be Custis Long, Miss

97

Iona MacSorley would like a word with you. I'd be Marty Link, the ramrod of the Lazy B, and this here's Trooper O'Donnel, our boss wrangler. Miss Iona is waiting for the three of us at that tearoom across from the church."

Longarm said, "You can tell her I'll try. But right now I suspect I might have more pressing business. I have to have a look at a couple of strangers the town law picked up. If they're anyone I know, I might know where some of their friends are right this minute."

The two Lazy B riders fell in with him as he explained further on the way to the town hall. O'Donnel quietly asked why the three of them didn't just round up the two in the saloon and march them on up to join their pals.

Longarm sighed and waved the muzzle of his Winchester at the sort of sinister reflection the three of them made in a hat shop window as he asked, "Would you let a sight like that come at you without getting spooked, innocent or guilty?"

Link said he followed Longarm's drift. The three of them wore sun-faded denim and businesslike gun rigs. The hatchet-faced Martin Link had a ferocious beard, while Trooper O'Donnel's battered features were framed by muttonchops the color of rusty bobwire. On top of all that, Longarm explained, he was only guessing about the two still at large. There was no law of nature saying all those in town who weren't Russian Dutch had to be pals.

The three of them joined that same kid deputy inside. When Longarm explained, Sattler's young sidekick led them back to where, sure enough, two other gents dressed more cow than sodbuster sat morose as hell in a boilerplate box painted babyshit green.

One grinned out sheepishly at Longarm. The more experienced lawman nodded and said, "Afternoon, Fingers. Figured someone like you had a couple of his pals trying to make up their minds about some moves to be made mighty soon."

Turning to the others on his side of the bars, he explained. "This wayfaring stranger swept up unexpectedly would be the one and original Fingers Fawcett, just out of Jefferson Barracks after some hard time over a federal post office safe. Old Fingers can open your average combination lock without half trying and . . . right, this other poor simp would be Juicy Joe Walters, famous for knowing how to milk nitro out of dynamite without killing his fool self.''

The older Fingers Fawcett shrugged and said, "You ain't got anything on us, Longarm. Like you said, I just got out, and Joe here ain't got no dynamite on him."

Longarm nodded soberly and said, "It's early yet. Let me guess as to just what all four of you came here to set up. The winter wheat harvest is about to commence. All prices are rising this summer. So a heap of Eastern grain buyers have already started sending advance checks on wheat futures.''

He turned to the Mennonite kid and asked, "Are you with me so far?"

The kid said, "Sure. My Uncle Franz just banked the check he got from Chicago."

Martin Link didn't seem to grasp the notion. So Longarm explained. "Never mind why some grain dealers pay in advance, hoping the grain will be worth more by the time it's shipped. Just remember this is a small town with a bitty bank, already commencing to fill up with the just rewards of a whole lot of plowing last autumn."

Trooper O'Donnel objected. "You said those Eastern buyers only send checks as advances on the harvest."

Longarm said, "I'll explain along the way. I have to go arrest a couple more. If you gents would care to be deputized for an hour or so, there's bounty money on whoever robbed that other bank at the county seat a few days ago."

The two Lazy B riders exchanged grinning glances, and the young town deputy said he wanted to go with the three of them. But Longarm warned him he might catch Ned if he left those two birds in the hand unguarded. So the kid allowed he'd stay and guard them, but he wouldn't like it.

Walking back down to the Ganselblumchen, Longarm explained how any grain merchant's checks would be cashed by mail right off by any bank with a lick of sense.

He said, "It's sort of sad how many checks bounce when the futures market ain't going the way the wise-money boys were betting. But when you pay a farmer for his crop in advance, the money is his from the day he takes your check to his own bank."

Trooper O'Donnel soberly observed, "In other words, that innocent-looking little bank near the schoolhouse is overflowing with cash, even *before* that harvest these squareheads keep talking about!"

It had been a statement rather than a question. So Longarm replied, "You gents are more familiar faces if they've been here any length of time. So what say you two go in the front way whilst I circle around to drift in from that beer garden? That way we'll have 'em covered from three directions when I tell 'em they're under arrest, see?"

They did, and that was the way it might have gone, had both those rascals been seated at that same corner table when Longarm strode in from out back, Winchester down at his side.

But there was only one, drinking alone. Longarm glanced at Link and O'Donnel, who'd entered from the front and taken up positions at either end of the bar. Link met his eye and shrugged. Longarm shrugged back and turned to bear down on the one left in the corner. Then O'Donnel yelled, "Longarm! Duck!" and Longarm would have, had not the one in the corner been slapping leather on him as he rose, teeth bared and eyes brimming with desperation. So Longarm could only hope that gun going off behind him was aimed somewhere else as he crabbed to one side and whipped his Winchester up, yelling, "Freeze!" and then, when that didn't work, bounced the cornered desperado off one wall to crash down through his own less effective gunsmoke. He'd missed the toe of Longarm's left boot by a good three inches.

Longarm turned in the ringing sudden silence to see another form, that of the missing corner conversationalist, oozing blood into the sawdust as he sprawled facedown between Longarm and the bar. Martin Link said, "He must have been in the crapper. It was Trooper here who got him as he was throwing down on your spine!"

Chapter 12

The English-speaking county board was disposed to let a Mennonite community handle as much as it could on its own, and as was often the case in remote parts, big froggies in the little puddle tended to wear extra hats. The only local member of the Kansas Bar Association served as the Sappa Crossing justice of the peace, the vet doubled in brass as deputy coroner, and the town's only banker could produce an undersheriff's badge the county have given him if he had to.

It still took almost until supper time to tidy up the shootout at the Gansblumchen.

Close to a dozen witnesses, from Zimmermann the manager to the town drunk, agreed on all but the petty details. They'd seen Longarm come in one back door, followed shortly thereafter from another back door by the older of the two cadavers over at Zuber's hardware and casket shop. Everyone agreed the one covering Longarm's back had been the first to slap leather and that Trooper O'Donnel had only shot him in the back as he was fixing to do the same to a federal lawman. They seemed more confused about the details after that. Folks usually were after they'd witnessed a gunfight. For the real thing was usually over a lot sooner than it took to describe it.

Gents who thought slow enough to describe a gunfight usually lost.

But nobody had call to doubt Longarm's version, since he'd been on that side of all that gunsmoke. They took the word of a well-known lawman and the wanted flyers in Werner Sattler's office that the dead men had been well known as well. Tiny Tim Breen and Slick Dawson, the one who'd drawn first behind Longarm's back, had been wanted on bank robbery, murder, and horse-stealing charges in lots of places. So the only mystery was just how they fit in with Fingers Fawcett and old Juicy Joe, who were still alive and well and full of beans.

Brought to the hearing from their patent cell out back, both known safe-and-loft men denied they'd ever laid eyes on either of the dead crooks. Moreover, they could both produce prison release papers, and defied anyone to prove they'd stolen an apple off a cart since they'd served their debts to society and been turned loose.

One of Sattler's other deputies had meanwhile found the washerwoman down by the creek who'd been providing room, board, and perhaps other services to the two dead men as they waited, they said, for some pals to ride up from Dodge. She stridently denied, in High Dutch, knowing either Fingers or Juicy Joe. She said she hadn't been paying attention to the ponies her paying guests had quartered out back with her mule. So far, the town law had only found two saddles to go with the four poorly cared-for mounts. Fingers and Juicy Joe were sure they'd last seen their own saddled ponies at the municipal corral, and threatened to sue for their full value if the infernal Dutchmen had lost them.

The mostly Mennonite town council cum coroner's sub-panel were more worried about that than Longarm. The experienced lawman and the one paid-up lawyer in the bunch agreed they could hold the rascals for a full seventy-two hours on suspicion alone without bending the Bill of Rights too badly. Meanwhile, it might be a good idea to get someone from the county seat to verify the two survivors had been at least somewhere near that bank over yonder around the time it had been robbed.

Stepping outside with his Winchester cradled in the late afternoon glare from the west, Longarm found himself in the company of Miss Iona MacSorley, who said she'd been waiting and waiting at that stuffy old tearoom.

Longarm assured her, "I wasn't aiming to be rude. Your hands and me got sidetracked."

She said, "I know. *Athair* will be so proud of them. I heard some of it inside once I'd been told what all the fuss up this way was about. What are we to do if nobody can prove those meanies robbed that bank at the county seat a spell back?"

To which Longarm could only reply, "Let 'em go. Nothing else we *can* do if we can't prove more than suspicion after seventy-two hours. It happens that way a heap. By definition, a sneaky crook leaves as few signs as he can. The two that were killed this afternoon were known to be gunslicks. They'd likely been recruited as backup. The two we have on ice are experts at opening safes, and nobody was watching when they cracked that bank safe in the dead of night. What was it you wanted to see me about, Miss Iona?"

She said, "I heard somebody took a shot at you earlier. I was going to suggest you come back to the Lazy B with me tonight, where you'd be safer. But I guess you got the ones who were after you, right?"

Longarm shrugged and said, "Mebbe." He had no call to voice all his suspicions to anyone before he had more answers. So he didn't. He said he meant to sleep out on the prairie after dark, seeing he could eat in town and needed neither a night fire nor more than a ground tarp in such dry summer weather.

Iona glanced at the sky to their west and said, "It's up to you. But we're fixing to have a glorious sunset, and I think I heard thunder in the distance earlier."

He said, "I noticed it's gotten cloudier. But those few clouds to the west were starting from scratch against sunny blue, and I suspect those Ruggles sisters have been setting off more dynamite to the north. Those corn fields they've been paid to rain on ain't more than a dozen miles by crow, and sound flies as straight across the sky.''

She insisted he had a standing offer covering room and board at her cow spread as she untethered her white pony and let him boost her up to her sidesaddle. She held her head sort of flouncy as she rode off down the street without looking back. He'd noticed she was used to having her own way. He wondered if that was all she found exciting about him.

He cut across the wagon ruts to a corner grocery and bought a bag of staples that would keep until old Helga got around to preparing them. He'd noticed that kitchen was getting sort of sour-smelling since the missing gunsmith's icebox had gone dry. He knew Dutch folks, high and low, favored sauerkraut and pickled everything else because it tended to keep without ice or smoke. So he hoped she wouldn't be too disgusted by canned pork and beans, bully beef, sardines, and plain old potatoes and onions in season.

She wasn't. When he marched in the back door to plant the big bag of vittles on the table she looked like she was fixing to cry. She said she'd be sore as hell if he didn't have supper with her, and then she did get teary-eyed when she read some of the labels and figured out what they meant in her own lingo.

Then she said something even more cheerful. She told him her own quarters were over Heger's carriage house out back. He'd let her move in when she'd gone to work for him. Longarm wasn't as sure it made up for not paying her any wages worth mentioning. Helga's reason for making supper on the far side of the backyard became clearer once they'd gone that far with the vittles and he'd noticed how much better things smelled.

Helga said her boss had ridden off somewhere with his one pony and two-wheel shay. So it came as no surprise that a certain amount of musty fodder and horseshit lingered in the air downstairs. Up in the converted hayloft it smelled much more like a lady's well-kept quarters. She'd spread lavender water and fresh-picked wildflowers about, but you could still smell an undercurrent of lye soap and elbow grease. She'd told him she hadn't much liked her earlier job cleaning house for another gal. But it probably felt different cleaning just as thoroughly for yourself. As she sat him on a cot to bustle with the grub across the spacious single room, he set his hat and Winchester aside and asked if she'd heard the one about Abe Lincoln's boots.

When she said she hadn't, he explained how a visitor to the White House had caught the president on the back stairs, putting new blacking on a pair of boots. When the surprised visitor had said, "Surely you don't black your own boots, Mister President!" old Abe was said to have replied, "Well, sure I black my own boots. Who's boots do *you* black?"

She didn't laugh. It reminded him of that time a real Russian lady had tried to translate a Russian joke into English for him. He felt a slight twitch below the waist as he idly wondered where that sort of warm-natured Russian gal might be right now as the sun declined in the west.

Helga's cast-iron range ran on coal oil, which she said she was running low on. She said there might be some left in the cellar across the yard. She hadn't poked about down there because it smelled so bad.

Longarm said, "I noticed. Airing it out only seems to make Heger's quarters upstairs smell worse. You did say you'd never met that wife of his in the flesh. Do you know anyone in town who might have really seen her leaving with that mysterious stranger?"

Helga shook her blond head with her back turned to him as she replied, "I am nothing knowing about Herr Heger's troubles *mitt seiner Frau*. When she in the door walk I would not know her. I don't think there will be oil enough for coffee also here."

He got up from the cot, saying he'd go see if there was any to spare in or about the shop. As he was leaving she gave him a key ring and suggested he lock up for the night on his way back.

He said he would and asked about all that stock, only guarded now by some hasty boarding-over. She said she'd left such stock as shells and cleaning fluid to the mercy of any prowlers, but hidden the more valuable guns in a broom closet with her fingers crossed, seeing she had no way to open the vault.

Longarm spied a bucket in the carriage house as he descended the steep steps. So he took it along and filled it with water from the garden pump before he went on over to the back entrance to the shop.

He sniffed uncertainly as he carried the bucket of water and that lantern back down to the cellar. He'd noticed in both the war and some Indian fighting that what folks ate the day they died had a lot to do with how they stunk afterwards. He still recalled the horrid shape a bunch of dead Na-déné had appeared to be in after a shootout down by Apache Pass a spell back. An army surgeon had finally figured out why they'd rotted so strangely. The hungry Indians had been eating desert buckthorn berries, which tasted insipidly sweet and contained a vivid dye that turned your blood vessels the color of black cherries without hurting you otherwise. Those dead Indians had sure looked odd.

Setting the bucket of water down, he rummaged about through cobwebs and old mason jars filled with ominous blackness until, sure enough, he found a square can of that Standard lamp oil of Ohio. He set it on the steps with the lantern before he slowly and thoroughly slopped well water over every inch of the dirt floor. Then he hung the trimmed lantern up, put the oil can in the bucket, and went up to lock the back door and head back to the carriage house.

He left the bucket where he'd found it and carried the lamp oil up to Helga—just in time, she said. He started to warn her to put out her stove burner before she poured more oil. But despite the odd way she talked she was a smart as well as industrious housekeeper.

She served him warm pork and beans and what she called *Bratkartoffein* at a small table near her dormer window. They tasted like fried spuds to him. They were both hungry enough to let the coffee catch up with them. As they ate, he didn't tell her about soaking the dirt floor across the way. It was a trick army looters and Mexican raiders used. But he didn't think he ought to mention anything buried under a dirt floor while they were eating, and it was going to take a spell in any case. You dug where you still saw a damp patch after the rest had dried. Soil that had been disturbed sucked up and held far more spilled water. But even with the cellar door ajar it would take hours for any such pattern to show down there.

They had coffee with a dessert she improvised from canned tomato preserves, brown sugar, and bread crumbs. It tasted better than her droll recipe. The light inside was getting tricky as, outside her dormer window, the sky to the west was turning ominously lovely.

Helga said the sunset was *wunderbar* after all the cloudless and sudden sunsets they'd been having. He found himself humming a few bars of an old trail song.

She dimpled across the table and asked him to sing the words to such a *schöne Melodie*.

He smiled sheepishly and said, "It's just a verse allowing how it's cloudy in the west and looking like rain, whilst I left my slicker in the wagon again. Such songs go on forever without saying a whole lot. Riders make 'em up as they just keep riding with no end in sight."

She commenced to softly sing in High Dutch. It was a haunting old melody, but of course he couldn't follow a word of it. She sang a spell anyway, and then she explained it was about this soldier boy in her old country who'd warned a fair maid he only meant to love her a short spell.

Longarm said he'd heard some soldier boys were like that.

Helga said this particular one loved the fair maid just one

109

year, then decided it wouldn't hurt to love her another year, and before he knew it he'd loved her forever.

Longarm cautiously said he'd heard some fair maids were like that.

Helga wrinkled her pert nose and said the song must have been made up by a man, because it took so many things about maidens fair for granted. She said it would have served that soldier boy right if the gal had sent him packing when they'd made love as long as she'd said he might.

Longarm laughed and marveled, half to himself, "She cooks too!"

She didn't follow his drift. It was odd how some of the folks from her old country could speak English like everyone else while others, try as they might, sounded like vaudeville comics making fun of the poor Dutch greenhorns.

There came a low rumble across the sky. Longarm sighed and said, "If that ain't the Ruggles sisters, I'm facing a moist midnight out on the lone prairie. I'd best see if I can scout up another hayloft here in town."

She murmured, "We shall *donnerwetter* before midnight have, Custis."

Then she reached across the table to timidly place a hand on his wrist as she added, "Don't leave. I have fear, even if it wasn't so wet outside going to be!"

He shot a thoughtful glance at the one cot across the room. Helga followed his glance, fluttered her lashes, and murmured, "There is for me alone more than room enough. So what if both of us in the middle tried to sleep?"

He took her hand more warmlly in his own as he said he doubted either would get much sleep that way. Then he felt he just had to say, "About what that soldier boy told that fair maiden in that old song . . ."

But she was already on her feet, holding his one hand in both of her own, as she tugged him away from the table, gasping, "Forever is for human flesh so short, and one hour is better than never. Why are you teasing me so, Custis? I will better try to understand your jokes if you will better try to understand a woman's needs!''

So they soon discovered she needed it most the old-fashioned way with a pillow under her already ample padding. He'd noticed she seemed to have a romantic streak before he'd gotten the two of them undressed and ready to get down to brass tacks. But she kept hugging and kissing like they were in a porch swing with her legs crossed instead of wrapped around him tight, as she combined the innocent schoolmarm kissing of a country gal with some bumps and grinds that would have made one of Madame Emma Gould's gals envious.

He learned not to tongue her when she sobbed she wasn't that sort of a *madel*—and damned if he wasn't starting to *follow* her High Dutch.

They said that famous British spy Richard Burton could learn a new Hindu dialect over a weekend by going to bed with what he called a "horizontal dictionary." The queen kept refusing to knight him because he kept saying things like that in mixed company. But old "Nigger Dick," as his fellow officers called him behind his back, had warned of that Sepoy Mutiny, if only his commanders had listened, because he could pass for a native and often did, carrying on scandalously with all those Hindu dancers who taught him how to talk as dirty as any Hindu.

Helga didn't smoke in bed, although she seemed to enjoy toying with his old organ-grinder as they cuddled close for their second wind.

She'd been right about her cot being sort of snug for two.

He lit a cheroot for himself as he stared up at the slanted ruby red ceiling, mildly surprised it was still so early. He could hear a lot of conversation coming down the sleepy trail at them, for it was way earlier than he usually turned in, and there were limits to what a man could do in bed with a gal, however bouncy, who'd only do it the old-fashioned way.

Blowing a thoughtful smoke ring, Longarm mused aloud,

111

"I can't go picturing the one left as a bewhiskered cuss with a vaudeville accent. There's no natural law saying it has to be Wolf Ritter to begin with. And Ritter's been running loose in this country, doubtless spending his own nights with horizontal dictionaries, and could sound like a natural cuss if he puts his mind to it."

She murmured, *"Bitte?"* Which likely meant she was having trouble following his drift again.

He explained. "Neither of those two locked up by the town law could have shot out your shop window earlier. They were rounded up by your Werner Sattler as they were lurking down by the creek. They swear they were fishing. They were likely looking for their pals, Tiny Tim and old Slick. That washerwoman we figure all four were staying with backs up their stubborn story. I wonder why."

Helga gave his tool a playful quarter turn as she said, *"Ach,* so smart you are! You at the table said those two in the saloon acted as if they were not you expecting!"

He took another drag on his cheroot and agreed. "The numbers tally to at least five with cause to disapprove of me. First one morose individual pegs a shot at my back, out front of your shop. A few minutes later Sattler's boys grab two obvious strangers when they see 'em hanging about down by the creek with no local address they care to give. Their two pals the local deputies *failed* to spot as suspicious were acting more innocently in that saloon. From what I heard passing through, Tiny Tim was for riding on whilst Slick Dawson was hoping to bail their pals out. Like you said, neither of 'em spotted me as the law when I was drinking in the same room with 'em. They only recognized me as trouble when I came back with a Winchester acting more troublesome!"

She kissed him under the ear and said, "The one who *does* know so much trouble you are was the one who chased you inside to meet me, so *freundlich*! So it is he who has your *Washfrauh* too afraid to tell the truth, *ja*?"

He shrugged a bare shoulder under her unbound blond hair

and said, ''That washerwoman could be just another hard case with no love for the law. To get such folks to talk, you have to convince 'em there's something in it for them. We couldn't budge her at the hearing this afternoon. There's not a dime's worth of bounty posted on the two birds we have in the hand. We can't tempt her with what was posted on those two more serious killers, now that they've been killed. I've told Martin Link and Trooper O'Donnel how to put in for the rewards on both those bad apples. My boss doesn't approve when we do it, and *somebody* ought to collect on their otherwise worthless hides.''

She began to stroke him faster as she coyly decided there might be some value left in *his* hide down yonder.

He said, ''Let me get rid of this smoke and position you a mite strategically then. It ain't that I don't enjoy swapping spit with you, pretty lady. But now and again it inspires a man to new heights when he enters at a new angle.''

She pouted that she liked to be kissed at the same time a lot, and bitched about a mean boy she'd almost married before she found out he had unnatural vices.

As he rolled her on her side with her smooth soft back to him, she gasped, ''*Nein!* I will not in the Greek manner hear of it!''

Then she arched her spine and gasped, ''*Ach du Lieber!*'' as they both enjoyed the way his semi-erection slid into her smooth wet womanhood with her behind against his belly. So a good time was had by all as she decided that that seemed to be another proper position, although vulgar enough to feel wickedly exiting, like Gypsy music in church.

In the end he had her on her hands and knees, taking his full thrusts dog style, as she swept the rumpled bedding with her wildly tossed blond hair and moaned and groaned in High Dutch that sounded awesomely dirty. The room was almost dark by then. So he kept catching flashes of sweeping hair and pale bare buttocks as, outside, summer lightning proceeded to flash regularly. Then, as he was pounding her to glory, hail

113

started pounding on the roof right over them. So he was mighty surprised when the buxom blonde suddenly shot forward, spitting him out like a big watermelon seed, and gasped, "*Ach!* Someone is coming!"

Longarm grunted, "Yep, me," as he dropped down atop her to ram it back in—he thought. She sobbed, "Not in me there! Can't you hear it? Someone in the shop is around fucking!"

Longarm was already off her and listening, hauling on his jeans as he decided, "She's got good ears too. Or mayhaps she's better at the night creaks of familiar surroundings."

She groped for him in the gloom, saying, "Don't go. I have *angst* and do not now hear anything!"

Longarm said, "That's because he's already busted off enough of that window boarding to get in. It's likely a thief. I was afraid my hasty carpentry would be tempting."

He strapped on his six-gun and then, since she'd started to cry, he groped in the duds on the floor for his watch chain, hauled out his watch and attached derringer, and placed the wicked little gun in her frightened right fist, saying, "Make sure it's somebody you'd like to see dead before you even point this bitty thing. For it may seem small, but it packs two awesome punches."

Then he rose on his bare feet and said, "Hold the thought. I'll be right back if we've been imagining things. Where's that key ring, honey?"

She said, "On that table near the door. Don't leave me here so scared to feel! We can try it in the Greek manner if you will stay here only!"

He groped his way to her key ring, and headed down the steep steps and across the yard through the storm, grateful to the Ruggles gals if this was their doing. For while it had to be playing hell in the wheat fields all around, the widely spaced but seriously thudding hail served to mask any footfalls of a barefoot boy with a key ring in one hand and a six-gun in the other.

He crouched in the storm on the back steps as he slowly turned a key in the backdoor lock, braced for nasty surprises even though he knew that the big vault hadn't been visible from the kitchen.

As he cracked the door open he heard someone whisper, "What was that?" deeper in the darkness. A louder, more assured voice replied, "Stray draft from somewheres. Told you it was going to rain fire and brimstone tonight. Knew Heger never gave them the money. Got the soap in place. So hand over that dynamite juice and . . . Careful, you butterfingered . . . *Jesus!*"

Longarm threw himself out of line with the doorway and hit the kitchen floor as the darkness was rent by a thunderous blast! His breath was sucked out of him by the shock wave through the air as the whole building bucked on its foundations. Then it got deathly quiet, save for the soft steady dripping of something soggy stuck to a wall somewhere in the smoke-and-nitro-fume-filled darkness.

Longarm gingerly raised his cheek from the waxed floorboards and softly muttered, "He told you to be careful, you poor butterfingered bucket of blood and guts!"

Chapter 13

It wasn't easy and some buttons were still loose, but Longarm was coming in through the back door again as Werner Sattler and some of his deputies were climbing through the busted-out front of the shop with more light to shed on the subject.

Longarm joined them, Winchester down at his side, as one of them held a lantern high and retched in the side room just behind the front shop. Longarm swallowed hard. He'd seen worse in the war, but there was little more than two pairs of bloody boots and blood all around to show where at least two men had been standing. The naked and partly skinned cadaver jammed in a far corner, stuck to the walls in a seated position, had apparently been a fat woman with gray hair.

Longarm said, "I heard. Sounded like dynamite, or nitro-glycerine. The laundry soap wedged in the door grooves of yonder vault tells a tale of tinhorn safecrackers who didn't know what they were doing!"

Sattler pointed at the fat cadaver in the corner and said, "That was Brunhilda Maler, the washerwoman those other dead crooks had holed up with down by the creek. I remember when she got that gold tooth in the front."

The younger deputy holding the lamp gasped, "*Lieber Gott!* That pair of Texas boots with Mexican stitching I remember

Hans Decker away for sending!''

Sattler swore softly under his breath and told another deputy to go check on another deputy named Decker. He added as an afterthought, ''See if Josef Lehrer is all right. The last time I saw him today, he was wearing a striped shirt that matches a rag I see stuck to that other wall!''

As the deputy tore out the front Longarm tried the handle of the vault, saying, ''Seems undamaged, save for some chipped paint. It's just as well they blew themselves up instead. They must have had a heap more nitro than professionals would have thought they needed. What's the sad tale of them fancy Texas boots, Marshal? You say one of your own sent away for 'em?''

Sattler sighed and replied, ''Good help is hard to find. If I was right about that scrap of shirt material, it adds up to malfeasance. All my deputies knew we suspected old Brunhilda of sheltering the safecrackers. They went and made a deal with her. It's a good thing for us she tagged along to make sure she got her cut. I don't know how I might have pictured this mess with just my two dead deputies to hint at what might have happened.''

Longarm nodded soberly. ''It does add up to wayward youths and a cunning old trash woman biting off more than they knew how to chew. You don't learn to handle high explosives by just reading about 'em in the *Police Gazette*. But what do you reckon they were after in yon vault? Hadn't we agreed old Fingers and Juicy Joe had come to town to crack your *bank* vault?''

Sattler hesitated, then said, ''Hell, you're the law too. But I hope you understand this is a sensitive secret.''

Longarm snorted in disgust and allowed he was a part-time reporter for the *Denver Post*.

The older lawman must not have thought he meant it. He said, ''The three of them must have had more faith than some of us. I warned the elders they were dealing with an outsider. But they thought Heger, being popular with some of his customers over in Cedar Bend, could catch more flies with honey than with vinegar.''

''You're talking about those rainmaking Ruggles sisters,'' Longarm said flatly.

Sattler nodded. ''That short sharp storm's blown over as suddenly as it began. But it's the simple truth that those *Hexen* have not gone away and left our wheat alone.''

Longarm said, ''I doubt that summer hail was occasioned by dynamite in the sky or dancing about with snakes. But how was Horst Heger going to drive those weather witches away so sweetly? With money instead of honey?''

Sattler nodded soberly. ''Eighteen thousand dollars and change, collected a few dollars here and a few dollars there from all the Brethren homesteaders. We'd heard the corn growers to the north had posted less than that in escrow, hoping for rain. We didn't *want* any rain, with our own fields ready to harvest. You see, if the ground—''

''I know about reaping machines getting stuck in mud,'' Longarm cut in. ''Let's stick to all that money Horst Heger was supposed to bribe those Ruggles sisters with!''

Sattler made a sweeping gesture at the battered walls of the tiny shop and asked, ''Do you see either Heger or the money here? Do you think those rainmakers would take the hardearned tithings of this whole *Gemeinschaft* to stop making rain, and then go on and curse our fields with *hail*?''

Longarm said, ''That storm passed over before it could have done enough damage to ruin anybody, and your wheat growers have sold a heap of futures, meaning they get paid the same for a poor crop as a good one, right?''

Sattler nodded down at the cadaver in the corner as he said, ''That's where the real money would have been tonight. The three of them must have thought Heger would have been dumb enough to skip out on all his bills and leave the money he never gave those *Hexen* in his deserted shop!''

As if to prove that last statement wrong the shopgal, Helga, came in to join them, bodice laced prim and blue eyes big as saucers as she marveled, *"Herr Gott! So Unordnung und wer ist das im Ecke?"*

Longarm was surprised how much of that he could follow as Helga stared in horror at the mangled lady in the corner. He told her not to look and suggested she cut some cake out in the kitchen, for it was shaping up to be a busy night.

He didn't know how truly he'd spoken until that kid deputy tore back in to pant that neither Decker nor Lehrer seemed anywhere to be found. Then he made it worse by adding, "Kurt Morgenstern just gathered a posse over by the creek!"

Sattler gasped, "He can't do that! Kurt's a damned blacksmith, not a lawman!"

The Mennonite kid said, "I don't think Kurt and those others care. They say they're riding over to Cedar Creek to put those rain *Hexen* out of business one way or the other! They say they paid for it to stay dry, not to have it hail. So they want their money back too!"

Longarm didn't ask where they were going as he chased Sattler out the front way. He said, "My hired ponies would be behind that Morgenstern's smithy, assuming he's half as honest as he expected Heger to be. You go on and get your own self going and with any luck I'll catch up with you along the way!"

Sattler didn't argue. They just ran their separate ways, and so it wasn't long before Longarm was splashing across Sappa Creek on the paint, alone in the renewed moonlight—and what in blue blazes was the matter with this fool pony?

Horseflesh, like humanflesh, was heir to the same agues and cramps that made it easier to run at some times than at others. It was too late to go back for the other pony by the time he was back on the higher range of the Lazy B and still hadn't been able to get the paint loosened up to lope right. You could do a heap of damage to a mount if you pushed it too hard with a sprained ligament, swollen frog, or whatever. So he cut off to his left, hoping it wasn't too late at night, and saw to his relief that all the front windows were lit up as he rode toward the Lazy B home spread.

Iona MacSorley and her ramrod, Martin Link, came out on the veranda as Longarm reined in, saying, "Got to get over to Cedar Bend on the double and this pony's gone lame. Could you help me out with a fresh mount?"

Iona told Link to see to it, and he lit out across the yards as if she'd snapped his ass with her riding quirt. It seemed possible she had. But she acted as if butter wouldn't melt in her mouth as she invited Longarm inside while her hands took care of more mundane chores.

He politely declined and headed after Link afoot, leading the paint by its reins. As she fell in beside him, pouty-lipped, he explained he was on his way to prevent possible harm to some other gals. Iona asked which one he was sparking.

Longarm laughed and assured her he hadn't sparked with either of those rainmaking gals, which was the simple truth as soon as you left Helga out of it.

As they got to the stable, Link and Trooper O'Donnel were leading a bigger roan outside on its rope halter. Link said, "Rocket here can carry a man your size to glory. She stands sixteen hands and if you see a fence in your way, she'll jump it for you."

"Irish bloodlines," Trooper O'Donnel chimed in with just a hint of smugness.

Longarm just got cracking to get his saddle and bridle aboard the big roan mare. As they helped him, the two Lazy B riders who'd been such a help in that saloon offered to ride along with him if he wanted to wait up just a few minutes.

He said he doubted there'd be shooting if he got there soon enough. Then he forked himself aboard the bigger pony and lit out to get there soon enough.

They'd been right about the roan's strength and speed. She'd have been a pleasure to ride nowhere in particular. She tore on across a rolling sea of moonlit grass with her hooves pounding steady on sod rendered just right for pounding by that passing summer storm. Cows and night critters scattered as they tore through the night, but the ride was so steady Longarm was able to think as clearly as if he'd been seated in a rocking chair, mulling over all those odd goings-on. The only trouble was, mull as he might, he couldn't figure out what in blue blazes could be going on!

Chapter 14

You didn't have to be Mexican to engage in Mexican stand-offs. An even number of prudently hot-tempered men from Sappa Crossing and Cedar Bend had lined up along a prairie rise just south of Cedar Bend to shake fists and brandish weapons. The mostly native-born barley or corn growers who needed rain stood their ground, on foot, in a sort of infantry skirmish line. The mostly Germanic wheat growers had reined in short of the bonfires along the rise to sit their nervous mounts nervously as, out in the middle, a dismounted clump of leaders, whether elected or self-appointed, seemed to be arguing about who the Good Lord and the Thunder Bird should love the most.

As Longarm rode in with his badge pinned on his denim jacket, he called out, "I wish you gents would quit looking daggers and glance up at the starry sky above us! That line squall was a natural fluke that anyone but an Eastern green-horn or a stubborn Dutchman would expect more than once a summer!"

A Cedar Bend man Longarm recognized as one of old Dad Jergens's deputies bawled, "Try to tell that to these fool fur-riners! Such rain as we got with that hail was barely enough to lay the durned dust, and the hail played hob with our poor parched cornstalks!''

Kurt Morgenstern, the usually more friendly smith from Sappa Crossing, growled loudly, ''Our quarrel is not with you Yankee homesteaders. If you want to plow at the wrong time for this climate, we agree it's a free country. But it's not *supposed* to rain at this time of the year, and we don't *want* it to rain at this time of the year. So we paid those Ruggles sisters to stop trying to make it rain, and it rained, and we want our money back!''

An older Cedar Bend man yelled, ''That ain't the way we heard it! All we got was a mess of busted down corn stalks. So we ain't paying them that rain bounty the bank was holding in escrow, and neither one of 'em is down in the valley behind us!''

The Cedar Bend deputy declared, ''They left earlier this evening, before that hailstorm. For they'd run out of dynamite and none of us would extend 'em any more credit!''

Morgenstern demanded, ''Why won't you let us pass then?''

Longarm announced, ''Same reason you boys from Sappa Crossing would guard your wheat fields from night riders, Kurt! As a paid-up lawman I'd be honor bound to side with anyone being unlawfully and unfairly trespassed until such time as his federal homestead has been proven and deeded fee simple! But the man just told you those rainmaking gals ain't hiding in any of their corn fields, and I for one believe him. I never would have asked them to scare my stock with dynamite to begin with, and no offense, you've all been acting mighty unscientific.''

Morgenstern demanded, ''How can you say that? One of my customers showed us the newspaper article saying they had a government patent for their rainmaking balloon!''

Longarm shook his head wearily and explained. ''You mean you saw how a bearded wonder who *calls* himself a scientist patented a method of setting off dynamite under a balloon without losing the balloon. The U.S. Patent Office demands a working model if you're trying to patent a perpetual-motion machine. But most of the time they'll issue you a patent on most anything that just might work, whether anyone would ever want one or not.''

He saw he had their attention. So he got out a cheroot and lit it to give them more time to think before he continued. "The drugstores are filled with patent medicines because, next to mixing up a medicine that cures something, nothing beats a patent number on the label as a reason to buy. It's the mixture in the bottle that you get the patent on. The contents don't have to *do* anything. I hope by now you've all seen how much rain you get using Dan'l Ruggles's patented sky bombs. Whether those two gals were bombing the sky with either his permit or knowledge is moot. Like I told the older one earlier, it ain't a federal offense to practice quack science.''

"What about *Hexerie*?" asked an old country wheat grower as if he meant it.

Longarm replied, "If you're talking about witchcraft, that's even more impossible. I've never understood why grown men and women can't show the common sense of Miss Esmeralda, that Gypsy gal in the yarn by Mon-Sewer Victor Hugo.''

That made some of them laugh uncertainly, and nobody seemed to follow his drift. So Longarm explained. "They brung this Miss Esmeralda before the king to fess up to being a witch, seeing everybody knew Gypsies had such secret powers.''

Some of the men in the crowd allowed they'd heard as much.

Longarm blew smoke out both nostrils and said, "Miss Esmeralda had more sense. She asked the king, if he had secret powers, if he'd prefer to wander the world homeless and ragged-ass, having poached hedgehogs for supper and swiping apples for dessert. The king didn't have to study long to follow her drift. He was a smart old bird, for a king. But then this witch hunter who'd been turned down by Miss Esmeralda

125

thought up some more charges. Witch hunters can always come up with more charges, since proving you ain't a witch is tougher than proving you ain't never coveted thy neighbor's ox or ass. But had Miss Esmeralda pled innocent in *my* court, I reckon I'd have had to agree with her simple defense.''

He heard men on both sides muttering that his words made sense, to the extent they had anything to to with that damned hailstorm.

Then old Werner Sattler finally caught up with Longarm, not saying where on earth he'd been, as he called out, ''You had no right to call a posse together without asking me, Kurt. What are you trying to do, a range war start? *Das gefallt mir nicht, Dummkopf!*''

Longarm saw Martin Link and Trooper O'Donnel along with the six or eight Sappa Crossing riders with Sattler. He didn't ask whether they'd all met up on the range or whether the Sappa Crossing boys had detoured to recruit some more regular Americans.

Kurt Morgenstern called out, ''We're not here to fight with these spring planters, Marshal. We gave Horst Heger good money to pay those *Hexen* off and since they didn't stop, we want our money back!''

Old Werner snorted in disgust and said, ''*Es tut mir leid,* you have all been golden bricks sold by that *Berlinisch schwindler*! He never gave any money to those American girls. He never paid the back wages of poor Helga Pilger or also Katz the *Lebensmittelhandler* for over two months already! He *said* he would try to pay those Ruggles sisters off with the money your committee collected, Kurt. Then he rode away with it, leaving everyone the bag to hold!''

Another Sappa Crossing man protested, ''You mean he abandoned his shop and all those guns?''

Sattler shrugged and said, ''He wasn't selling enough of them to pay his bills. It was not at all wise to let him get his hands on so much cash all at once, *nicht wahr*?''

Trooper O'Donnel piped up, his English a contrast to the

Mennonite version Longarm was getting used to. "I can tell you how pressed he was for cash. I dropped by a week or so back to have him outfit my store-bought S&W with ivory grips. He asked me to pay in advance. He said the factory back East wouldn't send 'em C.O.D. any more."

There came a thoughtful rumble from men on both sides who'd dealt with the missing gunsmith. A Cedar Bend man called out, "He was never the same after his woman run off on him. Did you get them ivory grips, Trooper?"

The Lazy B rider grinned in the moonlight and called back, "I sure did. From Miss Helga when she filled my pre-paid order. You can ask her if you like. My point is that her boss was cutting things close to the bone, and your marshal here tells me you laid more money on him than his business would take in all year if business had been better! No offense, boys, but that was just plain dense!"

Kurt Morgenstern asked the Cedar Bend lawman defensively if they were sure Horst Heger hadn't paid off those Ruggles sisters.

The deputy shrugged and said, "If he did, they sure spent it all in a hurry. They left here ragged-ass-broke and begging us for eating money as far as the railroad."

The burly smith wanted to ride on after them anyway.

Longarm raised his voice to announce, "I have some wires to send. I'll ride after them and see what they have to say in McCook. I don't want anyone else butting in. So now I'll be riding on, and anybody following this child by moonlight will be in considerable peril, for like the Indian chief said, I have spoken!"

Chapter 15

The difference between your average livery mount and a good cow pony was the difference between a schoolyard bully and a full-grown prizefighter. The roan mare loped with a mile-eating rotary gait. Her left hoof hit the sod ahead of the right, then her left and right rear hooves landed in the same order so her powerful haunches could launch her forward for another quick round. Rocket was a good name for her.

The late night air was chilled by that brief storm, and the melting hail had left cool clear water puddles almost anywhere man and mount wanted to rein in for a five-minute breather. So they made time that old Pony Express would have been proud of, and got into McCook as the sky was pearling lighter to the east.

To save tedious conversations about other horseflesh at the livery, Longarm stabled old Rocket behind the hotel near the Western Union. Then he hired himself a room near the bath, and went across the way to send a mess of telegrams.

Knowing he wouldn't have any answers for a spell, he found an all-night beanery near the railroad stop and ordered waffles with plenty of butter and sorghum syrup to go with his ham and eggs.

As he sat at the counter smiling back at the waitress, who'd dressed up as a Harvey Gal but flirted with the customers anyhow, he got her to jawing about current events in the prairie railroad town. Hardly anybody heard as much small-town gossip as a hash slinger in an all-night beanery. She said some railroad yard hands had been jawing about a real looker camped in a Gypsy wagon over on the far side of the water tower, just off railroad property.

Longarm changed the subject to other strangers who might have had a coffee or more while waiting for a train. It was easy to see the sass took considerable interest in such customers. It was a shame she was so flat-chested and had such a silly grin. But even after he identified himself as the law and encouraged her to think harder, she failed to recall anyone answering to his description of either Wolf Ritter or that missing gunsmith, Heger. She wasn't the first one he'd talked to who'd pointed out that neither description was all that astonishing. Men around forty, of medium height and build, with dishwater-blond or light brown hair maybe going gray, had a coffee or even a glazed donut all the time while passing through town.

He decided he'd have a glazed donut with his second cup of black coffee too. She'd been able to tell him that someone who sounded like a Ruggles sister had made it to town ahead of him. So neither Ritter nor Heger could have ridden in whooping like a Texas badman while shooting at street lamps.

He left a dime tip to show he'd noticed how friendly she'd been, and went back outside in the dawning light to find his way afoot to at least one big red wagon.

It was light enough to make out distant colors by the time he'd waded through trackside weeds past the water tower. So he knew those two bulky wagons farther out than he'd expected had to be the rainmaking expedition.

As he strode in, he found the younger one who seemed to do all the work seated on the fold-down steps of their circus quarters in the lighter of the two. There was no sign of the mules they'd had back near Cedar Bend, and the gal looked

130

as if she'd been crying. Her feet were bare and her light brown hair was unbound as she sat there in a dragon-splattered kimono of fake silk, poking at a dead cookfire with a stick. As she spied him approaching, she looked up with what he read as mixed hope and dread.

She said, "You're that lawman who was talking to Roxanne down by Cedar Bend. Has she been arrested?"

Longarm ticked the brim of his hat at her and replied, "Not as far as I know, Miss Rowena. You gals made good time across the prairie with these big red wagons. You must have been driving like the devil in the flesh was after you."

The gal smiled wanly and replied, "When you fail to work up as much as a heavy dew after weeks of corn killing drought, it's not too safe to loiter about. We were halfway here when that damned line squall blew out of the west last night. I wanted to go back and see if we couldn't at least parlay that into a few square meals. But I guess Roxanne was right. You quit when you're ahead when your hydrogen acid runs out and you owe half the merchants in the county. She said when she went off with the little money we had left that she'd bring back at least some coffee and staples. I was half asleep when I agreed to it. Now I can see what she meant by quitting while she was ahead."

Longarm said soothingly, "Ain't hardly anything open in town at this hour. I didn't think you were kin to the real Dan'l Ruggles, but you really are sisters, ain't you?"

Rowena laughed wryly and replied, "Not exactly. We met as cell mates less than a year ago. I was doing six months for shoplifting. She'd served half her jolt for pulling the old Gypsy switch on the wrong alderman's wife. But you've had time to find out all about us, being as professional in you own way, right?"

Longarm didn't want her to think he wasn't omnipotent. So he had no call to ask how two adventurous young gals had come by all this rainmaking flimflammery. He said, "I told your sister—I mean Miss Roxanne—your confidence game wasn't covered by federal statute. I want you to keep that in mind as I ask you a more serious question. I ain't after you on any charge, and such money as you may or may not have betwixt you is none of my beeswax. Do we understand one another so far?''

The disconsolate gal in the thin kimono shrugged her sort of pretty shoulders and asked, ''What's to understand about money we don't have? I told you we were run off as nearly flat-broke failures. We were so sure it just *had* to rain after weeks and weeks without any.''

He said, ''Welcome to the High Plains in summertime. I know about the escrow fund set up for you ladies by the Grange at Cedar Bend. That was the money you never got because it never rained before you ran out of gas for your balloons. Do you have any of that dynamite left, by the way?''

She said, ''Only a few sticks. Roxanne thought she might be able to trade them and the mules for food in town. Maybe she did. There was a morning train through here just before dawn. Have you ever listened to a railroad whistle in the wee small hours, wondering who was on it, going where?''

Longarm said, ''I heard that same whistle a mile or so out on the prairie, and wondered much the same, only not about Miss Roxanne. To get back to my reasons for pestering you like this, I was told an old boy from Sappa Crossing had been commissioned to pay the two of you good money if it *didn't* rain. His name was Horst Heger. Middle-aged Dutchman, albeit not one of them Mennonites. Your turn.''

She shrugged and said, ''Do I look like anyone's just handed me one whole silver dollar? Some of those Dutch homesteaders to the south did ride over to *cuss* at us when we were sending up our fool balloon. Lord knows why. We thought all farmers wanted rain. But the Cedar Bend boys wouldn't let them near us. I don't recall anyone called Horse, for land's sake. So where's all this money he was supposed to give us?''

Longarm said, ''I'm still working on that. I just sent a mess

132

of wires, hoping for details nobody around here seems able, or willing, to help me out with. I figure I might have a better grasp on some of 'em before this day is done. Meanwhile, I've had a long hard night and a man gets some rest when he gets the chance. So I thank you for clearing at least one of those details up, and I'll get out of your way now, Miss Rowena.''

She told him he wasn't in her way as she faced some worries of her own. But he ticked his hat brim again and strode off anyway as, behind him, the young gal in the kimono seemed to be sobbing her lonely heart, or empty stomach, out.

Longarm knew better. It wasn't as if they paid him all that well, and the young sass doubtless deserved a hard time. But once he was back on McCook's main street, he sauntered into a grocery he found open and had them fill a paper sack with simple but hearty canned goods and a fair grade of coffee. Nobody but a regular Don Quixote would spring for genuine Arbuckle Brand he'd never get to drink.

When he asked if there were any other groceries open that early, he was told there were none and that he was their first customer of the day. So it seemed it took a Ruggles sister to know a Ruggles sister and there old Roxanne went, with all their money and some dynamite as well! You could hardly blame little Rowena for bawling a mite.

As he strode back along the railroad tracks with his gun hand free, as was his custom, two burly gents in railroad overalls cut him off, one packing a baseball bat while the other backed his play with a sawed-off Greener 12-gauge. So Longarm called out, "Howdy. I ain't looking for a free train ride. I'm just out to deliver some grub to a lady, and I'm sorry my route takes me across this stretch of your right-of-way."

The one in the lead with the baseball bat smiled wolfishly and said, "We'll see how sorry we may have to make you, pilgrim. You say that sack's for that whore camped down the line with them circus wagons?"

Longarm stopped just out of easy batting range and replied, "She ain't a whore. She's a flimflam, and only one of them

133

wagons is a circus wagon. The other one's a gas generator, only right now it's empty and easier to move. I would be the law, federal, and both wagons are on federal open range right now, if it's all the same to you.''

The yard bull growled, "Anyone can say they're anything. Where's your badge if you ain't nothing but a saddle tramp in duds no fancier than our'n?''

Longarm wasn't about to have both hands full at the same time in such uncertain times. So he hunkered to set the groceries on the path before he rose back to his considerable full height with his billfold open in his left hand to flash badge and identification.

The yard bull peered hard, blinked, and said, "Great day in the morning if you ain't that one they call Longarm! I surely hope you understand we were only doing our job, Deputy Long!''

Longarm put the billfold away and hunkered down for the groceries again as he said, "Doing it right too. I respect any man who takes his job serious, and we've agreed this path runs across railroad property.''

He rose again and, as they made way for him, added, "Don't spread it about, but the ladies camped down the line may be government witnesses at a federal trial in the near future. So I'd be obliged if nobody pestered 'em before they're ready to move on.''

The railroaders swore on their mothers' heads that nobody would go anywhere near those red wagons while they drew breath. So Longarm went on and, finding nobody seated on those fold-down steps this time, strode almost to the back door before he saw the naked lady giving herself a sponge bath at the counter inside.

She saw him at the same time and hunkered down, with her knees and elbows only managing to hide the most private details of her willowy young body.

Longarm moved out of the line of sight, calling out in too cheerful a tone, "I brung you some grub to tide you over till you figure out your next moves, Miss Rowena. I'm sorry I surprised you like that. I didn't see nothing important and I'll be on my way now."

He meant it, but as he turned away she called out to him, and so the next time he saw her she was standing in her doorway with that kimono back on.

She demanded to know the meaning of that sack on her steps. Longarm moved back toward her, explaining, "You ought to be able to sell two wagons for enough to carry you on to fame and fortune in other parts, Miss Rowena. But meanwhile you have to eat, and when a body with something to sell is really hungry, some buyers can tell. I had to sell a good pony for eating money one time, and I sure hate to see a skinflint take advantage of an empty belly."

She said he was either a saint or out to take advantage of her empty belly, adding in a hangdog tone, "Not that I have much choice, and it's not as if you're old and ugly."

He shook his head and said, "Being a crook has ruined your faith in the rest of mankind, Miss Rowena. It was you who just called me back, as I recall. You paid in advance for barely two dollars' worth of coffee and staples by clearing up that matter of a missing gunsmith. Leastways, you've convinced me he never gave you ladies the money he was supposed to. You'd have both been long gone by now if you had the small fortune that seems to be missing along with Horst Heger!"

He started to turn away again. She called out that she had no matches to start another cookfire. As he ambled back to give her some, she said she wanted to hear all about that gunsmith she'd never heard of, and asked if he couldn't at least have some coffee with her.

So Longarm wound up gathering more kindling while Rowena got out her fancy coffee percolator and filled it with canteen water and a cheaper brand than he'd have chosen had he known he'd be invited to drink some of it.

On the prairie you found windfallen branches about as often as your found lost silver dollars. But there was plenty of

135

dried sunflower stems, wind-cured tumbleweed, and such to crumple up under well-dried cow pats. But it took such a fire a time to boil water. So it was a good thing Rowena shared his wicked tobacco vice. They got to sit on the steps side by side and share a cheroot for a spell as he brought her up to date on all his tearing back and forth across the prairie of late.

But she was too hungry to hold out for coffee with her beans, and so she opened a can and ate them cold with gusto. Longarm had figured grub you could eat cold from the can might be best. He didn't tell her what a swell breakfast he'd just had when he declined her kind offer to share her meal.

By the time they were sharing some coffee she was thinking clearer on a fuller stomach, and decided Horst Heger had indeed skipped out on his pals with all that money. She started morosely at the telegraph poles alongside the nearby railroad as she said she knew the feeling.

He shrugged and said, "I've run across such tales of woe a heap in my travels. Folks who never set out to betray a trust just find it too tough to be trustworthy, feeling broke and desperate with temptation winking and pointing down the primrose path."

She murmured, "That bitch said I was her one and only friend in this cruel world. Those wheat farmers have seen the last of that bribe their pal was supposed to offer Roxanne and me, unless . . . Oh, no! What if that Dutchman *did* get through to Roxanne, behind my back, and *that* was why we left Cedar Bend so suddenly? I never actually heard any of those corn growers telling us to leave!"

Longarm blew a thoughtful smoke ring at the dying fire near their feet before he said, "Works either way. You've about convinced me you haven't been eating regular as your average rich lady. But forget anything they ever told you about honor among thieves. Old thieves tell that whopper to young thieves.

You'd know better than me how well you really know your older pal, Miss Roxanne.''

Rowena laughed, in an oddly dirty way, and softly replied, ''I'd been led to believe we were more than pals. Adventurous women can't afford to take too many men into their confidence. But I guess when you get right down to it, anyone with confidence in you is a mark to a confidence woman, but damn it, she told me she really loved me!''

Longarm whistled softly and quietly said, ''I'm starting to see why she left you feeling so teary-eyed. I've noticed how many shady folk seem to wind up more than friends. I've never decided whether you get that way being locked up so long with nobody of the opposite gender, or whether owlhoot riders who can't afford to be too trusting find the notion more practical.''

He blew another smoke ring and continued. ''I recall reading about this Greek general, Alexander, who ordered his army to satisfy one another as best they could at night rather than let barbarian gals wander all about their fortified camps after dark. That was what the old-time Greeks called these white folks who behaved a mite like our modern Indians, barbarians. But our army gives you a dishonorable discharge if they catch you in the same bunk with another trooper, Indian country or not.''

''I'm not a lesbian,'' Rowena pouted. Then she added, ''At least I don't *think* I'm a lesbian. What do you call a girl who only pleasures herself with another girl when, like you say, they have her locked up or surrounded by stupid hayseeds?''

Longarm shrugged and replied, ''Practical? It works both ways, you know. Your erstwhile partner in pluviculture could have been scratching her own itches the same way and, now that you've run out of work, lit out with the proceeds. But if it's any comfort to you, I doubt she'd have been so mean if she'd had all that money from Horst Heger. When I talked to her she struck me as smart, and it would have been dumb to

137

strand you like this if she was running for the hills with *real* money.''

Rowena was too smart herself to need diagrams on any blackboard.

She nodded thoughtfully and said, ''Fifty dollars or less would have taken us both far and wide before she ducked out on me, and so you'd never have been having this conversation about her with me.''

Longarm didn't answer. There was no call to say she was right when they both knew it.

Rowena borrowed the cheroot and took a deep drag on it before she handed it back and said, ''Well, thanks to you and the way my brain is starting to tick again, I suppose I'll just sit tight till I'm sure she's not coming back. Then I'll get dressed and go into town to see who'd like to buy all this useless gear and be on my way back East. I was planning on trying my luck as a stage dancer before Roxanne sold me this bill of goods and taught me some other bad habits. Maybe it's not too late for me and the stage.''

Longarm had finished the cheroot. He ground it out in the dirt with a boot heel and declared, ''I'm sure you'll make a great stage dancer. You've sure got the build for it. It's been nice talking to you, but like I said, I was up all night and I have a hired bed waiting for me at my hotel, so . . .''

''What's wrong with catching a few winks here?'' Rowena asked, bold as brass. ''I mean, we've plenty of room inside, with Roxanne gone and all.''

He laughed incredulously and said, ''But I thought you were a lesbian!''

To which she demurely replied, ''Maybe I am. Why don't we find out?''

Longarm searched his mind for a reason not to, decided he'd wind up sore at himself in either case, and helped her up those steps by playfully pinching her firm bottom.

The innards of her circus wagon were partitioned into two rooms, with the smaller one in back the bedroom. He saw what she'd meant about the space her missing pal had once taken up. The bed filling most of the chamber was ample for two, and it was the only bed there was.

Rowena was on it, naked and giggling, before he could even shed his hat and gun rig. But he sat down and she helped him shuck the rest in no time, and then they were both in the center of the bed, atop the quilts, and she was starting to cry some more. So he stopped just in time to ask what in blue blazes was wrong now.

She said, "I'm sorry. I'm trying to respond like a sweetheart, but my last man abused me and scared me, and it's been a while since I've done it with *any* sort of man!"

He didn't offer to roll off and get dressed. He didn't like to make promises he couldn't keep. But he did lay side by side with her in the nude and kiss her, more gently, in the soft rainbow glow from her small stained-glass skylight.

She kissed back, less shyly and with more tongue, as he let her get used to his strange body pressed to her own. She didn't resist as he ran his free hand down between them to part her pubic hairs with two fingers and softly strum her old banjo. She tried to return the favor and then, finding herself with a delicate hand filled with throbbing cock, marveled, "Oh, you're already hard and yet so considerate! That other brute made me suck him hard and then he'd shove—"

"I don't want to hear," Longarm said, shushing her with a warm wet kiss as he commenced to strum faster in jig time. As he did so Rowena gasped, "Oh, Lord, you're making me so hot, darling!"

So he just rolled into her welcoming love saddle, and it sure felt swell to sink his raging erection into its overdue reward with his eyes closed and two young gals taking turns up and down his shaft with their tight hungry love maws. But he remembered who he was supposed to be doing it with when Rowena suddenly gasped, "Roxanne! We weren't expecting you back."

Longarm didn't stop. He might have, with a gun to his head, but he was fixing to come as he craned his head to smile sheepishly up at the older and darker gal in the doorway and said, "Morning, ma'am. I would stand up in your presence but, just now, that might be sort of embarrassing to both of us!"

Roxanne laughed harshly.

Rowena wasn't able to stop moving her hips either, but she was sobbing as she declared, "I wasn't messing with a mark, darling. I thought you'd run out on me and this one is the law!"

Her older and darker lover demurely replied, "I know who this is. Albeit he had his pants on the last time we spoke. Heavens, will you look at those muscles ripple. How is he hung, honey?"

Rowena gasped, "Gloriously! And I'm comingggg!"

That made two of them. So Longarm wasn't keeping track of anything but the sweetest tightest pussy in the world as Roxanne was explaining how she'd sold their mules and had a possible buyer for this particular wagon.

As she got in bed with them, naked as a jay, she said, "Nobody I tried seems to have any use for the old signal corps gas generator. Why don't we go sixty-nine while he takes turns pronging us or, better yet, throws a good old-fashioned long-donging into the survivor?"

Longarm wasn't too sure he followed their drift. But he made a grab for fresh meat as Roxanne literally rolled him off her younger pal.

The more fleshy and voluptuous Roxanne kissed him back, but then she shoved his hand away from her hairier crotch, purring, "Don't be so impatient. That prospective buyer isn't coming to look this wagon over until this afternoon, and you could obviously use a breather!"

That was the simple truth. So Longarm reclined on one elbow with a bemused smile as Roxanne took his place with Rowena. It was sort of interesting to watch the way lesbian gals went at it when neither had a dick.

At least, they surely *acted* like lesbian gals. They kissed a heap, and then Roxanne started kissing her way down Rowena's slender form, dark hair trailing across heaving breasts and excited belly as the older gal cocked one shapely thigh over her partner's to settle down in her face like a biddy hen fixing to hatch something.

So a good time was had by both as Longarm watched, feeling ever more inspired as the two of them gave one another some experienced and far from delicate licking.

From the way they were both moaning and groaning as they slurped, it seemed up for grabs who'd be coming first. But as the older gal must have known, and Longarm should have guessed, the less controlled younger one came first, sobbing aloud, "It's not fair but don't stop!"

So the smoldering Roxanne gave her a few good licks, and then she rolled off to lay spread-eagled between her two bed partners, saying, "Whee! I'm right on the edge but I won! So let me call you sweetheart, cowboy!"

Longarm's old organ-grinder was feeling mighty edgy as well by then. So he chortled, "Powder River and let her buck!" as he mounted her and thrust home, hitting bottom, and Roxanne gasped, "Keerist! You might have warned me, Rowena!"

But the younger gal was sitting up, pawing at Longarm's bounding bare butt as she sobbed, "Hurry, hurry, do hurry, and then do it to me some more!"

Longarm couldn't answer with Roxanne swabbing his tonsils with her tongue as she gyrated her bigger hips in jig time with his long-donging. How had he ever thought anyone else had the best damned pussy in the world when *this* one was obviously it?

Of course, once the three of them had shared an afterorgasmic cheroot and he was dog-styling Rowena while the friendly child ate her older mentoress, she did feel a tad tighter. So then he had to put it in the moaning and groaning

141

Roxanne some more to make sure, and in the end he was damned if her could decided whether he enjoyed hot pulsating wetness or wiggly smooth tightness more. The grandest thing about women, bless them, was that nine out of ten of them were worth screwing, while that tenth one was worth it as a change of pace.

Chapter 16

No lawman with the brains of a gnat would have let himself fall asleep among thieves, and Roxanne had said that prospective buyer was due to show up any time after noon. So neither gal seemed to feel insulted when Longarm finally hauled ass out of there walking funny.

He made it back to his hotel, forced himself to take the time for a bath down the hall, and flopped bare-ass and alone across his hotel bed to catch forty winks through the hotter half of the day.

He felt way better after close to six hours' sleep. Longarm arose around sundown to shit and shave, pay his hotel bill, and inhale some steak and mashed potatoes with plenty of black coffee downstairs.

At the Western Union he found answers to some of those earlier wires waiting for him. None of them told him all that much at first glance. He wadded them up and put them in a breast pocket of his jacket to go over again later. For as anyone who'd ever taken out a bank loan could tell you, it was easy to miss serious shit in the small print.

He picked up a sack of feed on his way to get old Rocket. As they helped him saddle and bridle her, Longarm lashed the trail rations to the saddle, balancing the Winchester's boot on the far side, and told the perky roan, "We ain't fixing to stop for conversations about your species along the way, Rocket. For I've a weak nature around women and we're in a hurry."

He led her outside in the gloaming, tipped the young stable hands, and mounted up, saying to old Rocket, "I make her a day's cavalry ride if we push on through to old Helga and that swell carriage house without stopping anywheres along the way for more than a trail break. I'll get you back to the Lazy B on my return swing, as I redistribute all you ponies."

Rocket didn't argue. Once they were south of the railroad tracks he let her have her head, and she loped as if she'd felt cooped up in that stall all day. She likely had. Mankind and horseflesh got along so well because a healthy horse enjoyed running across firm grasslands as much as most folks liked to ride.

But by the time they were even with her home spread, Longarm was a mite tempted to swing over and see how that paint felt about carrying him the rest of the way. For old Rocket was commencing to show the effects of her sportive gallop the night before.

It was only in Ned Buntline's Wild West Magazine that true-blue cowboys rode one true-blue steed at least as smart as a math teacher. A well-founded beef outfit kept six or seven mounts for each human on the payroll. That way a man could get a hard day's work out of a pony without permanent injury. He felt guilty about pushing another man's pony this hard two long lopes in a row.

On the other hand it was after midnight by then, and Sappa Crossing lay almost within an hour's ride downhill. So he pressed on, letting old Rocket walk every other furlong, till he had her in Heger's snug carriage house, with Helga yelling things like *"Wer is das?"* down the stairs at them until he told her it was him, and then she wanted him to get right up stairs and into bed with her.

He chuckled fondly and told her he had a few less pleasant but more important chores to tend to first.

He tethered Rocket by the trough, unsaddled her, and rubbed her down with some handy sacking as she enjoyed some water and oats, in that important order, lest she bloat her fool self.

Then he picked up a manure shovel from another corner and went across to the gunsmith shop's back door in the moonlight. He cussed when he recalled Helga's key ring. But the back door wasn't locked, bless her loss of interest in a boss who'd never paid her.

He went down to the cellar, lit that same lantern, and regarded the now dried-out dirt floor morosely. Save for a few tiny low spots hither and yon, the infernal floor had dried out evenly. You could smell stale piss and long-lost food scraps better now. But aside from being sort of sloppy as he worked at yon tool bench, the missing Horst Heger hadn't hidden a dead wife down here after all.

Upstairs, in bed with Helga after the pleasant discovery that neither Rowena nor Roxanne had the best little pussies in the world after all, he told Helga about his experiment in the cellar across the way, and added, "He could have buried her under this carriage house and he could have buried her out back in his yard. But a man with a dirt-floored cellar he could work in with a constitutional right to privacy would be a total fool to bury her anywhere else."

Helga shrugged a big soft shoulder and said, "I told you she had off with another man *abluafen*. We have more serious something to talk about, Custis."

He cautiously asked what seemed more important than at least two missing persons. She said she'd been offered her old job back, and he agreed cleaning house for modest wages, room, and board had waiting here for Horst Heger beat.

He said, "They have a Western Union up in McCook. So by wiring all over I managed to establish that that horse and shay that Heger kept down below was left at a livery over to the county seat by a late-night customer who never came back."

145

She asked if that meant her boss had hopped a train from there.

Longarm said, "Nope. They have a Western Union wire strung there, but so far, they've just been talking about a railroad spur to pick up all the grain hauled in to the county dealers and freighters. I never asked whether they haul it north or south to the rails from over yonder. Hauling grain more than fifty miles wipes out your profit. But like I said, that ain't my problem."

He took a thoughtful drag on the cheroot they were sharing and explained. "My problem is another missing man entirely. I'd be out of line searching for your missing boss if it wasn't possible the man they sent me after had something to do with his vanishing. I told you why I was so interested in that LeMat revolver Heger was trying to sell at too high a price. What I'd really like you to do for me would be to teach me just a few words of High Dutch."

Helga laughed incredulously and said, "*Ficken mich immer wieder!* Or at least let us until dawn do it. *Ich darf nichts* carry on with you this way if I am back to work in a Mennonite home to go!"

He gallantly told her he'd try to be a sport about the need to be more discreet. She said she'd been so afraid he might not understand, and wanted to prove she was still mighty fond of him by getting on top. So he let her, but kept pestering her for easy words and phrases in her own native tongue as she enjoyed a nice steady lope with his old saddlehorn. She thought it was funny as well as fun, and asked him who in the world he was going to use such baby talk on.

He said, "Ain't aiming to have a conversation. I've noticed, using way better Spanish, you can sometimes trick a suspect into an unwitting admission, or betraying guilty knowledge, by casually asking him something in his own mother tongue."

So after she'd tongued him some while bouncing faster, and he'd returned the favor by rolling on top, Helga managed to teach him a few things that might come in handy if he was

146

ever changing trains in that new Germanic Empire.

She said he tried too hard to gargle and spit, explaining most English speakers seemed to do that, even though nobody but those guttural Prussian Junkers really growled that much in High Dutch or Low.

He chuckled and asked, "You mean I could sound like a Prussian drillmaster if I put my gargles to it?"

She laughed and said he had his ramrod up the wrong way. Then she taught him how to snap *"Achtung!"* and suggested anyone who'd ever served Der Kaiser might be more inclined to pop to attention than a peaceful Mennonite. She had taught him some really dirty stuff to yell at folks by the time they just had to get some sleep.

He got enough to feel up to less pleasant chores by the time the good old gal had served him his breakfast in bed, and she tried not to cry as he got dressed and strapped on his gun rig. Neither one of them said anything about final good-byes as he kissed her at the head of those steep stairs and went on down them.

He made sure old Rocket had water in her trough, and promised he'd have her back out to the Lazy B as soon as he could. Then he headed up to the town hall.

As he entered Werner Sattler's office, the older lawman asked what had taken him so blasted long. "We're running out of time we can hold those safecrackers, Longarm. They've both been denying they ever even met that washerwoman or their two dead sidekicks."

Longarm nodded and said, "We figured them for old cons. I'm sure the Founding Fathers never had real crooks in mind when they carved that Bill of Rights in stone. There's a lot to be said for making us prove some damned charge or turning the rascals loose. But first things first."

He got out the wad of telegrams, peeled off the list he'd penciled on the back of one after picking at half a dozen, and explained, "I was so long in getting back because they have a telegraph office up in McCook and I wired high and low. I only know a couple of the old boys I narrowed it down to on sight. I'd like you to go over these names and say who might look anything like your average deserter from that Kaiser's cavalry. Did you know Junker comes from *Jung Herr,* or a young gentleman?"

Sattler snorted. "I thought it meant young lady. I know all the men I see on this penciled list. The only ones who'd fit Wolgang von Ritter's description can't be him. Those wanted papers say the Prussian killer has been in this country less than ten years. Our few middle-aged gray-blond homesteaders of average height and wearing beards have all gotten that way by being here longer."

Longarm frowned thoughtfully and pointed out, "I thought most of you Mennonites left the back steps of Russia around '73 or '74, at around the same time Wolf Ritter was fighting all those duels and mayhaps fixing to hop the same ship."

Sattler said, "When I said here longer I meant *here* longer. Here in Kansas. That Prussian renegade fought other duels, or just shot men, all over this country while the rest of us were civilizing one particular part of Kansas. Nobody on this list is a new arrival. Why have you listed them to begin with?"

Longarm explained, "They're old boys from around Sappa Crossing with money in the bank at the county seat. Your sheriff was proud to help the federal law with that, whether the county savings and loan was or not."

Sattler said, "That's no mystery. A lot of wheat growers buck their crops over there for sale. It's easier to cash a check in any town you bank in. And you just agreed those two in the back were out to rob our one country bank."

Longarm said, "I'd likely feel safer banking over to the county seat, across from the sheriff's department, whether I'd come by the money one way or another. Let's see if we can get Fingers Fawcett to help us out with Heger's vault, seeing we can't hold him much longer in any case."

Sattler took a key ring from a wall hook and led the way, even as he protested it was a waste of time for them and too big a break for a known safecracker.

He said, "We know Horst Heger was given that money to pay off those rainmakers. You didn't find it on *them,* did you?"

Longarm smiled wistfully at the image that conjured up as he said, "They didn't have nothing on them, last I saw of them. They were fixing to hold a going-out-of-business sale. That means Heger never went near 'em with that small fortune. Heger's horse and shay wound up in another town entirely. But he never put toad squat in any bank at the county seat, and he'd have driven to McCook if he'd meant to take it with him aboard any railroad train."

As Sattler jingled his keys along the corridor he insisted, "It would have been even dumber to leave the money in the vault at his shop and drive off to nowheres. I don't know how those kid deputies got the notion they'd find money there when they let that ignorant washwoman talk them into using that dynamite juice the professionals had left with her."

Longarm suggested they both ask. But when they got back to that patent cell and called the two crooks to the bars, neither one would admit he had any idea what they were talking about.

Longarm said, "Let's try it another way. We need to get into that vault neither one of you knows anything about. It's not nearly as tough a job as the bank vault you were interested in would have been. So we figure either one of you could crack it with one hand behind his back. Who'd like to spend another night in jail and who'd like to give it a try, with freedom to get way the hell out of these parts by sundown if he succeeds?"

From the way they both jumped at the offer Longarm suspected they could be sincere about never having heard of Heger's fool vault.

Longarm chose Fingers as the one least likely to bust windows in town. Sattler let him out, locked the cell again, and said he'd catch up as soon as he rustled up a deputy to hold the fort there.

As Longarm and Fingers Fawcett walked the short distance to the missing gunsmith's shop, the taller and younger deputy took advantage of the old crook's friendlier attitude to ask his opinion on the grim mistakes those novice safecrackers had made the other night.

Fingers insisted he'd never met the late Brunhilda Maler, but he volunteered that if he *was* a kid led astray by a wicked older woman who might have somehow got hold of some nitroglycerine, you weren't supposed to use that much of it, and you *never* held any loose in any bottle within a good fifty yards from any loud noises. The old con confided, "I've never liked to work with juice. If those awful crooks you keep asking me about were in town to bust into the bank, they only had that nitroglycerine along, in a sealed, totally filled bottle on a bed of cotton batting, as a last resort. The smart way is always the easy, least noisy way possible."

They got to the shop and simply stepped through the front window, seeing some damned kids had pried off half the boards. Once inside the gloomy shop, Finger sniffed and asked, "Jesus, what's that stink? It reminds me of this job I backed out of back East once I saw what the mastermind wanted me to do."

Longarm said, "Tell me about it later. The vault's this way."

Werner Sattler caught up with them in the blood-spattered chamber as Fingers was gingerly working the combination with one ear pressed to the steel while Longarm held a lantern high for him. When the town law asked what they were doing, Longarm warned, "Hush a minute so he can listen for the tumblers to click inside."

Sattler nodded and watched silently as the experienced old crook paused, wiping his sweaty fingertips on the front of his shirt, and said, "That's three. There's usually four to be fiddled for in this brand of lock. Let me get this old heart settled down. Like I was saying, this reminds me of the time I was recruited to open such a combination lock, leading into a family crypt. Seems they'd just put this old lady to rest with all her diamonds on, but I said no as soon as I literally got wind of what they wanted. You sure this gunsmith who ran off with all that money really ran off, Longarm?''

The lawman who'd recruited him said, ''Stop stalling. Let's open her up and see for ourselves.''

So Fingers got back to work and they did. The stench was incredible as the tight steel door swung open, and old Fingers ran into the kitchen to vomit out the back door. Werner Sattler just covered his mouth with a kerchief and stared goggled-eyed as Longarm raised the lantern higher for a better look at the horror that had been locked away for safekeeping all this time.

He soberly said, ''You'd know better than me if that was the suit Heger was wearing the last time anybody saw him alive. I don't envy your coroner, and if it's all the same with you, I aim to let the undertaker stuck with moving him find out just how much money he has on him.''

Chapter 17

But the local part-time undertaker said he'd never had to deal with a such a *verfault* cadaver, which was High Dutch for anyone left unembalmed that long in warm weather with no ventilation.

The dead gunsmith had burst his store-bought duds at the seams as he'd swollen up like that over a period of around a week. So it wasn't too tough to haul his duds out of the vault a yard or so at a time. There was usually a dry end to grab hold of. There wasn't any money to be found, in his pockets or in the soggy puddle of stinky body fluids left when they finally managed to scoop the half-naked form out on some planking to be covered with a tarp and carried away.

Later on, at the hearing held at the town hall, their part-time deputy coroner showed he was made of sterner stuff by declaring the late Horst Heger had did of gunshot wounds, a heap of gunshot wounds from .40-caliber to number-nine buck.

When it was Helga Pilger's turn, she said she couldn't say when all that gunfire had transpired because she'd never heard any shots.

When an old geezer on the panel implied she'd have had to be stone deaf, or in league with the shootist, to miss the dulcet sounds of four pistol shots and a shotgun blast from her quarters above the carriage house, Helga began to cry. So Longarm stood up and called out, "I know it ain't my turn. But *nobody* in that part of town heard any gunshots during the seventy-odd hours the deed could have been done!"

Someone asked if he was suggesting that the LeMat had been fitted with something to muffle the sounds of its fusillade.

Longarm shook his head and said, "Inventors keep trying to come up with a muzzle silencer. So far nobody has, and I doubt one would be much help with either a shotgun or revolver in any case. So here's what I think happened. . . . "

They dismissed Helga and told him to take her place if he felt so smart. After he'd done so, Longarm said, "I can't say whether Heger did so before or after you-all gave him that money to pay off those so-called Ruggles sisters. But along the way he recognized a wanted killer he'd once met up with in that spike-hatted army of Bismarck or his kaiser. It's been made to *appear* that it was when the notorious Wolf Ritter showed up on his doorstep with his notorious LeMat revolver. I ain't sure that's what happened. From all we know of Ritter, he's too slick and too rich to put such a giveaway on the market. I think he found out Heger had recognized him and wired my boss, Marshal Billy Vail, that he was somewhere in these parts, pretending to be somebody less disgusting in these parts."

A cowhand who'd drifted in for the free show exclaimed, "Hot damn! I see what happened! This Ritter cuss came in late at night with that swamping gun, killed the gunsmith with it, stuffed the body in that vault, and put the murder weapon in the window, like it was on sale, as he just walked off with all that money!"

Longarm said, "No offense, but that don't work. Remember the real Wolf Ritter, if he's in these parts at all, wouldn't want it known he was. After that, not being a Mennonite, he'd have had little call to know a clannish inner circle of wheat growers and town fathers, no offense, had gathered that dry harvest

154

weather fund. I'm the *law* and I've yet to get exact numbers as to just how much Heger may or may not have had on him when a party or parties unknown killed him, not in his shop but somewhere more private. There's a whole lot of open range all around, and those Ruggles sisters and their sky bombs would have excused any distant shotgun blasts.''

The deputy coroner brightened and exclaimed, ''I see it all now! After he'd killed and robbed poor Heger, Wolfgang von Ritterhoff smuggled the body into town, hid his body in the vault, and left the murder weapon in the window so that nobody would find it on him if he was questioned, *ja?*''

''Nein,'' said Longarm. ''The real Ritter wouldn't want to be suspected, whether he'd killed and robbed a soul or not. From his recent moves we know about, he's not getting any younger and he'd been trying to control his temper and settle down, not advertise. So suppose the late Horst Heger confided in a false friend he trusted, a Mennonite brother who'd know about all the money in that vault. What if *he* got Heger alone somewheres, an easier chore for a false friend than it might have been for an outlaw Heger had spotted around Sappa Crossing, and forced him to give the combination to his vault before killing him with another LeMat entirely and simply smuggling the body back into town under cover of darkness to rob the vault, hide the body, and leave the LeMat in the window at a price, assuring it would stay there until somebody smart enough to make the connection came along.''

The coroner gasped, *''Donnerwetter!* You mean to say one of our own set out to *abgekarteten,* I mean *frame* this other criminal among us?''

Longarm nodded and said, ''It worked pretty good, didn't it? Had me going until I began to notice loose strings I just couldn't tie to an owlhoot rider only partly accepted by a small farming community. I was asked to buy the late Horst Heger acting sort of peculiar too. Say he must have at least talked about Wolf Ritter and that LeMat to somebody he trusted. Why in blue blazes would he drive all the way to the county seat and send a telegram to my office clean out Denver way? Don't you have a county sheriff, an undersheriff sitting right in this room, or the town law—Werner Sattler?''

Somebody in the crowd said, ''That's right. How about that, Werner?''

Then somebody else said, ''Say, where's Werner? He was here a moment ago!''

Longarm was already on his feet, headed for the far doorway at a run as he drew his .44-40 with a wolfish grin, growling, ''Thank's a heap, you treacherous dumb bastard! I hadn't gotten to half the stuff I was fixing to bounce off your guilty conscience!''

Outside, as if he could read minds, a kid in a cap and knickers pointed at some settling dust across the way and yelled, ''He rode off that way! On another man's pony!''

Longarm could see that as he tore across the dusty street to find a cowhand war-dancing around in front of a hitching post, yelling his horse had been stolen.

Longarm asked what sort of pony they were jawing about. When the hand said he'd been riding a bay horse, Longarm ran over to a tethered cordovan and helped himself to it, yelling, ''Tell the owner I'm the law and I'll be back with both ponies, Lord willing and I don't get shot!''

Then he was after Werner Sattler, lashing his borrowed bronc with the rein ends as they tore between houses and over some fencing until they were out of the small settlement and galloping through ripe red winter wheat and to hell with the damage. For Longarm spotted Sattler out ahead on that purloined bay, going for broke catty-corner, with no regard for any neighbor's harvest.

Longarm was the bigger man but better rider. There was more to winning a horse race than just sitting there. So Longarm began to gain as he stood in the stirrups with his weight forward as they tore across the rolling wheat fields stirrup-deep in shattered stalks.

Sattler saw who was after him and twisted in the saddle to

shoot back at him. Longarm wasn't ready to return fire at that range. A man firing a Colt .44-40 from a standing position could hit another by shithouse luck at four hundred yards, but only nail him with certainty at fifty. Blazing away at full gallop made it even tougher, and it was a pain in the ass to reload without slowing down.

Old Werner was lucky, or good, as he sent some of his rounds way closer though wild. Longarm knew a wild round could kill you just as dead as a shot fired from a bench rest. On the other hand, if the son of a bitch was out of ammunition when a body caught up, there were still a heap of questions that could be answered.

Chasing him over a rise, Longarm saw they'd commenced to harvest the quarter section ahead. Dozens of men, boys, and a couple of gals in sunbonnets were gathering sheaves left by two mule-drawn reapers and running them over to a mechanical thresher powered by belting from a donkey steam engine set up a safe distance away. Nobody with a lick of sense wanted the firebox of a steam engine close to piles of straw and windblown wheat chaff.

The corrupt lawman and false-hearted friend rode between the two reaper crews and straight at the gap between the steam engine and threshing machine, yelling fit to bust in High Dutch.

So the steam engine operator released his clutch to drop the thick leather belting almost to the ground, and old Werner just tore through to the other side at full gallop.

Then the rascal at the controls snapped the thick power belt up tight, and Longarm nearly spilled as his borrowed cow pony shied to a halt and reared.

As he fought to regain control Longarm yelled, "Let me through, goddamn your eyes! I'm the law and he's getting away!"

A burly Mennonite elder with bib overalls, full beard, and pitchfork stepped between Longarm and the taut drive-belt to call out. *"Einen Augenblick, Mein Herr! Was wunschen Sie mitt unser Marschall?"*

Longarm yelled, "If your talking about your marshal, he's a killer and a crook!"

But now there were more stubborn-looking Mennonites blocking his path despite the gun in his hand, as their obvious leader said, not unkindly but firmly, *"Ich verstehen Sie nicht. Sprechen Sie kein Deutsch?"*

Thanks to Helga, Longarm understood part of the last. So he yelled, "Of course I don't speak Dutch to ignorant assholes! We're in the state of Kansas, not the back steps of Russia!"

Before he had to shoot anybody Longarm heard a commotion behind him, and turned in the saddle to see a dozen other riders from town coming to help or hinder him. Before he had to shoot any of *them,* good old Kurt Morgenstern yelled out in High Dutch and the harvest crew began to get out of the way. Morgenstern yelled, "Werner must have had *some* reason to bolt like that. But are you *sure* about all this?"

Longarm called back, "No. That's how come I want him alive. Tell that asshole at the steam engine clutch to let us through, damn it!"

So Morgenstern did, and they all followed as Longarm heeled the cordovan over the slack belting whether it wanted to go that way or not. But as he topped the higher rise beyond, Werner Sattler was not to be seen in any direction across the rolling wheat or prairie grass all around.

As Longarm reined in to stand taller in the stirrups, Morgenstern joined him there to demand, "Which way did he go?"

It was a good question. Longarm said, "North, east, or south work as well. Thanks to that squall the other night he aint raising any dust as he rides slower somewhere out yonder. He might be dumb enough to ride east to your county seat. He has a bank account yonder. Depends on how much of his ill-gotten gains he banked and whether he values his hide more."

The fatter and slower-riding banker cum undersheriff, who was supposed to be leading any local posse, caught up with them in time to overhear part of that. He puffed, "Werner has an account with us too. Not nearly as much as Horst Heger should have had on him, though."

Longarm asked how much was not nearly as much. When the part-time undersheriff and full-time banker estimated a modest four figures, the federal lawman said, "That's still a healthy bank account for a small-town lawman drawing, say, five hundred dollars per. And I know he has another account, like I just said, at the county seat. But I suspect he split that windfall with some partners in crime. That's how come I want to take him alive."

Kurt Morgenstern frowned and said, "I don't understand. Why would Werner have needed help in murdering poor Heger for that money he was holding for us?"

"That's too cute. You murder a man to rob him or you murder a man to shut him up. You seldom get to kill that many birds with one stone, and I've noticed in my travels that when there's two separate motives there's usually two separate crooks."

The undersheriff said, "I don't see two separate motives. We all knew that gunsmith had just been given some money to give to those two rainmakers. So Werner killed him for the money and tried to lay the blame on this Wolfgang von Ritterhoff, who may not have ever been anywhere near the scene of the crime!"

"Or vice versa," Longarm objected. "I'm pretty sure Horst Heger really spotted that other killer. My own office never would have heard about any of this if Heger hadn't wired us. The only way an honest man who wasn't familiar with American law would have made such an odd move would have called for some poor advice by someone who *was* familiar with American law."

They both proved his point by staring blankly at him. So he put away his six-gun and reached for a smoke as he explained. "Picture a gunsmith in a remote trail town recognizing a wanted killer. Heger had a mess of wanted posters in his cellar and the ones on Ritter may have jogged his memory or . . . never mind how he did it. He *did* it. So wouldn't he naturally go right to the town law with the information before he did anything else?"

Kurt Morgenstern brightened and said, "*Ach,* so! Werner suggested he keep it to himself and contact a more distant federal marshal than he had right here in Kansas because . . . *warum?*"

Longarm said, "To give everyone more time than they'd have had if Heger had wired Dodge the way he should have. The money the poor sucker had in his vault was windfall. Sattler could have only had one good reason for slowing down any outside help from arriving. Old Heger really must have been on to something. Wolf Ritter was a pal Sattler was covering up for. I mean to ask him why as soon as I catch him. I only know Sattler had no other reason to delay the search for a federal want. Wiring Denver instead of Dodge or, hell, Kansas City gave them an extra day or better to decide what to do."

Kurt Morgenstern said, "I vote we ride for the county seat. Even if he's not going for that other bank account, we can pick up more riders when you tell the sheriff about all this, *ja?*"

Longarm said, "*Nein.* You send a rider to tell the county law if you like. Sattler's just as likely to double back to Sappa Crossing if he means to risk a bank withdrawal at this late date. Besides, they never sent me after *him.* That sheriff you just mentioned has more jurisdiction over local robberies and killings. Wolf Ritter is the son of a bitch I'm after, and that wasn't him I was chasing just now!"

As he wheeled his borrowed pony, Morgenstern stayed with him, gasping, "*Herr Gott!* You mean that killer is still hiding somewhere among us, like a wolf in sheep's clothing?"

To which Longarm could only reply, "Don't know. Aim to

find out. I showed Werner Sattler a list of possible suspects. He naturally vouched for every one of 'em. He may have been fibbing. So I aim to ask others about the same gents, and this time I might have better luck.''

Chapter 18

He didn't. Everyone he talked to in Sappa Crossing, from the one barber to the Mennonite preacher, seemed to agree with their fugitive town law about such names as they recognized on Longarm's list. Few knew all the names. The clannish Mennonites could only vouch for their own brethren. Longarm hadn't expected a renegade Prussian Lutheran to pass for an all-out Mennonite. But as much as a fifth of the Dutchmen in those parts were from other sects entirely, and there were tradesmen and cattlefolk like the MacSorleys who weren't *any* sort of Dutch, High or Low.

Longarm considered more than one apparently plain American that barber recalled as bearded, of average height, with blond hair going to gray. But men who'd answer to that description were hardly as rare as virgins in a whorehouse. The barber said he'd have noticed if anyone ever sat in his chair with *dyed* hair or beard.

Longarm sighed and said, "I reckon I could tell, close enough to peer close at the roots of dyed hair or whiskers. You ain't a Dutchman, are you?"

The barber laughed and said, "Bite your tongue. I can manage a few words of the lingo. In this town you have to. But my people were from Welsh Wales, look you, if we want to go back far enough. I consider myself a plain old Ohio boy, if any of this conversation means anything.''

Longarm said, "It might. Nobody on this list described as any breed of Dutchman has left town since my office got that urgent message from the late Horst Heger. But some other bearded faces ain't been seen at the saloon and such of late. You talk to these squareheads more than most of us, pard. Do you reckon an educated Prussian officer might be able to speak English with no accent if he put his mind to it?''

The barber thought and decided, "Everybody has an accent. I can tell you're not from Ohio just by listening to you. Neither one of us speaks English like a York Stater. Your sneaky Prussian officer would have to speak anything with *some* accent, see?''

Longarm did. He nodded gravely and said, "I follow your drift, and I'm glad I was smart enough to come to you for advice. Now that you mention it, I have noticed an educated furriner *sounds* as if he has to be speaking with an accent, even if you can't place it, because he speaks with no accent at all, pronouncing every word exactly the way they tell you to in Webster's Dictionary!''

The barber smiled smugly. "So you could be looking for a bearded blondish man who speaks such perfect English he annoys folks, who left town after you got that telegram from our poor gunsmith.''

Longarm sighed and said, "I would if I could. But there ain't no such person, as far as anyone I've talked to can tell. Can you think of any customer who'd answer the overall vague description jawing at you in a *noticeable* American accent? I mean a thicker than usual Texas twang, a shut-my-mouth-you-all Dixie accent, or—''

"I know what you mean," the barber said. "Real folks don't lay it on the way vaudeville comics might. I can always tell a real Welshman from a teasing Englishman because my late Uncle Dai, from Cardiff you see, never in his life spoke half as Taffy. But I'm afraid you've come to the wrong barber

164

for help with Prussians pretending to be from Texas or Welsh Wales. I've been wracking my brains all the time we've been talking, and I just can't come up with anyone I can fit in that slot with a hammer!''

They shook on it and parted friendly. Longarm got a cool beer, at least, at the Gansblumchen saloon. Nobody there could put him on the trail of Wolf Ritter, and more than one suggested he'd been sent on a wild-goose chase. Had anyone but the late Horst Heger ever seen anyone in these parts who answered to the description on those wanted flyers?

It was a good question. All bets were off if the real Wolf Ritter didn't fit his official description. Such things happened. Witnesses gave conflicting accounts or just guessed at details they didn't really remember. There was still some argument as to whether Henry McCarty, alias Billy the Kid, was right-handed or left-handed. So what was a few inches either way, or a saber scar on the right or left cheek, to an owlhoot rider wanted for everything but the blue ribbon at the county fair?

Longarm had returned that cordovan cow pony, and said he was sorry as all hell. But he still had some horseflesh to reshuffle, Iona MacSorley had issued a standing invitation, and that paint would still be out at the Lazy B. So he went back to that carriage house, found Helga didn't live there anymore, and saddled old Rocket, telling her, ''Seeing I've been left in the lurch by one maiden fair and invited to sup with another, we'd best see about getting you on home.''

He stopped by Morgenstern's smithy to pick up that gelding as long as he was at it. It was better than even money he was through in Sappa Crossing. It made more sense to ask some more around Cedar Bend.

''You just want to get laid,'' he warned himself as he considered how much good old Dad Jergens and pretty Olive Red-Dog likely knew about the sons of bitches he was after. It made little sense for Werner Sattler to run for a nearby town where he was known, or for Wolf Ritter to try and blend in with native Americans, red or white. The renegade had only come to this broad land because there was a whole lot of it to run off across.

Longarm didn't see how one lawman was supposed to track at least a couple of crooks who had all that damned grass to ride across. But it happened that way at times. He didn't know where Frank, Jesse, or The Kid were planning to spend the coming night either.

He rode into the Lazy B dooryard late that afternoon. Iona MacSorley came out on her veranda to declare it would soon be supper time. Then she yelled until the ramrod, Martin Link, came running to see what she wanted.

She told him to take care of the two ponies, of course. So Longarm felt obliged to say, "I know the way to your stable, Miss Iona. Why don't you both let me worry about these brutes and then I'll wash up out back and join you?"

The pretty but pouty Iona said, "Marty's going to do as I say because he knows I mean what I say, Custis."

So Longarm dismounted and handed the reins to the foreman as he murmured, "I work for the same sort of boss. Only he ain't as pretty."

Link laughed indulgently and muttered, "Go on inside with her before she turns you into a toad. I'll have O'Donnel handle this chore."

Longarm nodded and followed what seemed a wise suggestion. Once in the house, Longarm found the imperious young gal and her baronial father seated by that big fireplace, as if to admire the cold hearth and all those swords and daggers over it. Iona said they'd all get their supper within the hour as old MacSorley poured him a dram of malt whiskey from a cut-glass decanter and sat down on the same sofa.

He'd poured one for himself and seemed to want to clink glasses. So Longarm let him, and assumed *"Air du shlainte!"* meant something a tad nicer than it sounded in *that* old country. It was hard to tell High Dutch or Highland Scotch apart when you spoke neither lingo. They both had those throat-clearing sounds you never heard in plain American.

It wouldn't have been polite to tell his host he sounded like a furriner of any sort. So he said the whiskey was good, and admired the cutlery around that shield above the mantel.

Martin Link came back inside as old MacSorley began to lecture Longarm on the warlike display. From the way Link and even the old man's daughter rolled their eyes, it was easy to see old MacSorley had given the same lecture before.

It was less tedious to a guest who'd never heard about targes, *sgean dubhs,* and claymores before. *Sgean dubhs* were those small but wicked daggers Scotchmen stuck in their socks. MacSorley said it was a point of honor to never draw from your sock unless you meant to kill somebody. The basket-hilted broadswords on either side of that round studded targe were what Scotchmen waved to make a point that might or might not be settled peacefully. When Longarm said he'd been led to believe those straight sabers were claymores, the older man pointed at the one old-time sword with a far longer blade and a hilt made for a man's two hands, saying that that was the true claymore or great sword of the Isles. He said mainland clansmen who spoke almost as much English as their Sasunnack enemies called their broadswords their claymores out of ignorance, or while showing off. He added that the correct Hebredian for any sort of sword was *"Claidheamh."* Longarm wasn't rude enough to say he didn't care.

Trooper O'Donnel came in to announce he'd unsaddled Rocket and draped Longarm's saddle over a rail to dry while he visited.

Longarm set his glass aside and rose to thank O'Donnel with a shake, adding, "Have a cheroot on me. We were just now talking about old country ways. Do you talk any of that Irish Gaelic, Trooper?"

As Longarm reached for that cheroot O'Donnel replied, "I used to know a few words. But my people spoke mostly English and I grew up on this side of the water."

Longarm got out the cheroot, saying, "Do tell? I didn't know the Irish Famine and Great Migration was that far back.

But you'd know Irish history better than me. I've been smoking this brand a spell and it ain't all that bad. *Haben Sie Streichhölzer?*"

"Trooper O'Donnel" was too slick to reply in High Dutch, but he did *nod* before he'd had time to think, and then he was staring down the cold unwinking eye of a .44-40 as Longarm quietly said, "Don't neither of you squareheads move a thing but your hands. I want 'em all *up!*"

MacSorley and his daughter were staring goggle-eyed as Longarm explained, "That wasn't exactly Gaelic I threw by surprise just now. I asked him casual, in his *true* native tongue, whether he had the matches to go with that smoke. Now would one of you be so kind as to relieve these two Dutchmen of their six-guns whilst I cover them?"

But before either could move, a familiar voice told Longarm from behind, "I have a better idea, Longarm. Drop *your* gun before I blow you in two with this ten-gauge!"

Longarm didn't have to wonder what that was sticking in his back so firmly. As he tossed his .44-40 on the sofa with a sigh he said, "We were wondering where you rode off to, Sattler. Right now, I sure feel dumb. But I wasn't sure anyone out this way but the foreman was High Dutch. Must have come in handy for old Wolfgang here. A real Irishman would have had to be a true top hand to be hired on as one."

Ignoring the lawman he had the drop on, the erstwhile town law of Sappa Crossing asked his grinning confederate, the fake Trooper O'Donnel, *"Was sonst noch? Was wunschen Sie?"*

Wolf Ritter smiled boyishly as he drew his own gun and said, "I think this will be more fun if we all speak English. As I told you out in the stable when I asked you to cover me, this one was much too clever for anyone's good, including his own."

He nodded at Longarm and demanded, "Who told you who I really was? Speak up. Don't make me resort to cruelty."

Longarm smiled wryly and replied, "Were you planning on kindness? Nobody had to tell me. You just now said I was clever. It was what we call the process of eliminating. I just kept eliminating and eliminating until here we are. If it's any comfort, *you're* pretty clever too. I reckon you learned to move so tricky under that sneaky Otto von Bismarck. I read how he tricked Louis Napoleon into guessing all wrong about his plans time and time again. A plain old crook would have simply killed Horst Heger. But you didn't know who he might have gone to aside from your old pal, the town law, here. So you razzle-dazzled that old LeMat you had no further use for to make it *appear* Heger had recognized a desperate drifter, in the hopes I'd assume you'd drifted on by the time I got here. You knew I'd take my time to get here, once you'd had Heger wire a distant office, or wired for him. I still have some loose ends to tie up.''

Wolf Ritter chuckled fondly and said, ''No, you haven't. I'm trying to decide whether it would be more amusing to let you join us for a last supper and watch as we all have this little slut for dessert, or whether it would be wiser to kill you here and now.''

Over at the far end of the sofa, Iona was huddled with her old *Athair,* trying in vain not to cry as the full meaning of this scene sank in.

Longarm said, ''I might have known you'd be scared of a grown man with only two guns backing your vaudeville villainy. You ain't really hiding any dueling scars under that dyed muttonchop down your cheek, are you? Fess up, as long as I'm fixing to die anyways. Ain't it true you paid a skin doctor to scar you a tad under ether? I was reading how some of you Prussian college boys get your he-man scars the safe and painless way.''

The renegade officer smiled coldly and softly said, ''It's a good thing you are not a worthy swordsman, you oh-so-clever peasant!''

Longarm shrugged and said, ''I had me some cavalry drill with the saber one time. Why do you ask? Are you offering me a fair sword fight?''

Wolf Ritter started to say something sneery. Then he frowned, smiled and decided, "Why not? It would be just the thing to work up a good appetite for food and other pleasures of the flesh. Werner, cover the kitchen with that shotgun. Martin, see nobody comes in the other way to disturb us as I give this lout a lesson in manners!"

Sattler protested, "I liked your first idea better!"

But Ritter pointed at the MacSorley sword collection with his own six-gun as he sweetly suggested, "Choose your weapon, my Yankee cavalier!"

So Longarm stepped over, unhooked that big two-handed claymore, and drew the clothyard of ancient steel from the cracked leather of its scabbard, saying, "I've always wanted to try one of these here crusader swords. Heavier than I expected, but the balance ain't bad."

The Prussian saberman laughed incredulously and helped himself to a more saberlike Highland broadsword, hefting it as he agreed the gents who'd made these lethal blades had known what they were doing.

Longarm asked if he meant to duel with a broadsword in one hand and that Schofield in the other.

Wolf Ritter smiled boyishly, holstered his six-gun, and shifted the basket hilt to his other hand, saying, "I naturally parry and thrust right-handed. *En garde*, you poor clumsy oaf!"

So Longarm, never having fought with a claymore all that much, got into a sort of baseball batting stance with the two-handed weapon as the smaller man with the lighter sword dropped into a more regular saber fighting stance with the tip of his own chosen weapon swaying like a steel cobra between them.

As Longarm stood his ground like a lethal baseball player, the renegade officer nodded thoughtfully and decided, "He's not quite so dumb as he looks. I am naturally used to dealing with *right-handed swordsmen*. I now have to consider how one takes on a *left-handed lumberjack!* That clumsy claymore only has to get in one solid blow and you might not stand so solidly afterwards!''

From his post near the front door Link said, "Left, right, *im Scheissenhaus* already! Shoot him and let's be done with him! We don't have time to play games here!''

The sadistic Prussian purred, "But we do! Nobody else can enter without permission of the foreman, and you haven't quit just yet. How are we doing with that Chinaman in the kitchen, Werner?''

Sattler replied, "He's cooking supper and keeping his mouth shut if he knows what's good for him. But I think Martin's right about our riding!''

Wolf Ritter didn't answer. He lunged at Longarm instead. Longarm had figured he might. So when the experienced but formal swordsman bored in with a formally flashing feint and slash, Longarm whirled completely around to his left, to come out of his spin with that monstrous Highland sword gripped right-handed for a normal attempt at a home run, just as Ritter's broadsword whistled through the space Longarm had occupied at the beginning of his diagonal slash.

The startled Prussian saw what had to happen next and tried to recover and parry, just a tad too late to really help, when a bigger man had already launched his own horizontal swing with a heavy three-foot meat chopper!

It felt to Longarm as if he was busting glass and chopping through a head of cabbage as the claymore in his hands snapped Ritter's blade to send flashing steel in one direction and Ritter's dyed head in the other!

Iona screamed like a banshee as the headless Prussian stood there spouting gore for almost a full second before the knees buckled. Then everyone was staring slack-jawed at the big bloody claymore Longarm had swirled up to thud into and hang from the ceiling rafters. That gave Longarm another instant to whip out his double derringer and fire it twice.

Once was enough to part Werner Sattler from his shotgun. Then Martin Link was screaming loud at Iona, gutshot, flop-

171

ping about on the floor while Longarm dove headfirst at the sofa, grabbing his six-gun as he rolled over the back and landed back on his feet in better shape to take charge again.

As Longarm covered the gutshot Link, the ramrod wailed, "I give! I give! For God's sake don't shoot me again!"

Longarm strode closer to kick Link's fallen six-gun clear across the room while, over in the kitchen doorway, the Chinese cook seemed to be softening Werner Sattler's remains with a rolling pin.

Longarm told him to cut that out, and asked old MacSorley if he had any hands who spoke more Gaelic than High Dutch. When the old Scotchman allowed he did, Longarm said he wanted guards posted all about and a rider sent to town to fetch the undersheriff, seeing the *town* law of Sappa Crossing had turned out so crooked.

MacSorley tore off to carry out Longarm's orders. Iona demanded, "Why make such a mess in here when you had that gun on you all the time?"

Longarm said, "No way to take out three armed men with two bullets. Can't you tally bang and bang?"

Then he hunkered down by the gutshot Link and declared, neither cruel nor mushy, "You're done for, Link. I don't like your color at all."

"*You* don't like it?" croaked the dying ramrod with such a wan smile that Longarm knew he'd worked his way past agony to numb acceptance.

Shaking the dying man's shoulder, Longarm said, "I can see they notify your kin and send you home in a lead-lined coffin, or we can feed you to the worms in potter's field. A lot depends on how much you'd care to clear up for my official report."

Link sighed and said, "I told them they were being too cute. But Wolfgang had to pile red herring on red herring until it's a wonder they didn't send in the U.S. Cavalry!"

Iona came over to complain, "Custis, that head you stood

over in that corner—it's making faces at me, as if it's still alive!''

Longarm said, ''It ain't. Marty here was fixing to tell us what in blue blazes that sneaky Wolf Ritter thought he was up to. Ain't that so, Marty?''

The dying man croaked, *''Mama, bist du es?''* as the girl insisted, ''Custis, that head in the corner just winked at me!''

Longarm said, ''Maybe it admires you. Get over here and take your dying boy's hand, Mama. I have to write down every word we can get out of him in English.''

So the dying Martin Link surprised them both a mite as he told his mama how he'd gotten his fool self in this fix. Iona was smart enough, or imperious enough, to reply in English each time he lapsed into the lingo of his childhood. Some of it surprised Longarm a lot. At the end he wound up nodding soberly at that head in the corner and telling it, ''You'd have pulled it off if you hadn't been so greedy and mean. But nobody would have been after you if you hadn't been greedy and mean to begin with. So I reckon it all came out inevitably in the end.''

Chapter 19

It was a good thing the night was warm and Mennonites drank in moderation. The crowd that rode out from Sappa Crossing had to be assembled in the dooryard, and old MacSorley barely had enough of that malt whiskey to go around.

The deputy coroner presided from the front veranda at a table the Lazy B hands had toted outside. Most everyone else got to stand or hunker wherever they could find the space.

Old MacSorley, his daughter, and the Chinese cook, in that order, had much the same tales to tell and didn't take long. But when they got to Longarm the deputy coroner declared, "I sure hope you'll do more for us than the previous witnesses, Deputy Long. For now one can picture the blood and slaughter inside this house this evening, but what *led up* to such a gory ending?"

Longarm stood before the panel with one foot on a veranda step and a fresh cheroot in hand so he could speak clearly as he began. "Once upon a time there was this hot-tempered Prussian officer I'd as soon call Wolf Ritter because that's what on most of the wanted flyers. He was such a mean cuss he even shocked the Prussian Army, and they were fixing to court-martial him because he couldn't get it through his head they wanted him to kill Frenchmen, not fellow officers. They don't lock up officers and gentlemen as they await a court-martial, so Ritter just ran for it. Made it to America and proceeded to pick fights for pleasure and rob folks for eating money.''

Kurt Morgenstern volunteered, ''Then Horst Heger recognized him when he came to Sappa Crossing, *ja*?''

Longarm said, ''*Nein.* Forget about Horst Heger till I get to him, and don't horn in unless you want this to be even more confusing.''

He took a drag on his cheroot to make sure they were listening to him tight. Then he continued. ''Before there was any such trail town as Sappa Crossing, while most of you all were learning the ropes up in Dakota Territory, Wolf Ritter was raising Ned in other parts with two lesser-known partners, a Dutch American kid called Martin Link and a wayward Mennonite you'd later know as Werner Sattler. But Ritter, being so mean and such a show-off, was the only one of the three who wound up wanted by the law by name.''

Almost as if they were singing a duet in harmony, the undersheriff and old MacSorley bayed about the foreman and town marshal being crooks.

Longarm took another drag as, this time, the deputy coroner told them to shut up and let the witness proceed.

Longarm said, ''As they doubtless recalled to their chagrin this very evening, pulling off jobs with a partner in crime such as Wolf Ritter tended to be needlessly exciting. And I've noticed heaps of owlhoot trail riders weary of the chase after missing many a warm supper or a good night's sleep in a feather bed without half so many things on one's mind. So the older Werner Sattler was the first to drop out. Being a Mennonite by birth, if not conviction, he found it easy to drop out of sight up Dakota way as he started to act more law-abiding.''

A church elder with a long gray beard objected, ''*Einen Augenblick, Jungen.* Nobody *ist* by *birth* a member of the Brethren. He must of his own free will as an adult be baptized!''

Longarm calmly replied, ''I stand corrected, but Sattler still found it simple to fade into the Mennonite scene. Then he

176

came on down Kansas way when the rest of you all hived off to form your own wheat-growing community. You made him your town marshal because he asked for it and nobody else of Mennonite persuasion wanted it. If any of you found him a tad worldly for your tastes, at least he was one of your own and he did seem to know how to handle a drunken cowboy when and if he had to. So in sum, for as long as there'd been anybody at Sappa Crossing, good old Werner Sattler had been established as the law, not an outlaw.''

Old MacSorley asked, "But what about my foreman, Martin Link? I asked for references when he came out from town to replace the one who'd left without notice and ... *Och, mo mala!* The town law vouched for him having an honest record, and what do you suppose ever happened to that *first* foreman I hired!''

Longarm suggested they stick to one mystery at a time and continued. "With one old partner established as the town law, and another doing the hiring and firing here at the Lazy B, Wolf Ritter saw his chance to vanish into thin air as he was being posted dead or alive all over this country. Anyone who'd ever served as a cavalry officer could wrangle cow ponies, and it was up to the foreman who had to be told to do what. So Mister MacSorley here had no call to doubt Martin Link when he was told he was paying those top-hand wages to a boss wrangler. So let's leave the three old pals getting fat and happy in these parts with nobody suspecting a thing.''

"Until Horst Heger recognized an old comrade in arms, *ja*?'' said that talkative Kurt Morgenstern.

Longarm shook his head and sternly warned, "I asked you not to horn in. Horst Heger had never served in any military unit with the renegade Prussian officer. If they had ever met, an outlaw on the prod should have been the first to recognize anyone. Ritter had been smooth-shaven and scar-faced as well as blond in their old country. Heger likely looked much the same as he ever had. He wasn't the one growing muttonchops and likely having his hair trimmed and tinted over at the county seat, or mayhaps McCook. We wrap up such details as we get out final reports. Suffice it to say, there's no call to assume Horst Heger knew beans about the three wolves in sheep's clothing. He had his own worries. Business had been slow and his wife had run off with another man. I found her to be alive and well, or at least alive and working in a house of ill repute, out Tombstone way.''

Morgenstern looked as if he fixing to piss his pants as he wailed, ''Then what did our poor gunsmith do to them? What *could* Heger have done if he didn't *know* anything?''

Longarm let the deputy coroner glare for him as he took a drag of his cheroot. Then he said, ''Nothing. Ritter, posing as an Irish hand called O'Donnel to hid his slight accent under a slight vaudeville brogue, had Heger order him new grips for his six-gun as a matter of fact. Heger's misfortune was that, despite his personal problems, you'd all done business with him at one time or another and decided he was an honest man. So once those rainmaking gals came over the horizon to threaten your winter wheat harvest with unseasonable rain, you thought, you collected a handsome payoff in hopes of a dry harvest. Some folks say kissing a frog might turn it into a handsome prince too.''

The undersheriff, seated to the right of the deputy coroner, said he'd counted the money, given receipts to the donators, and passed it on to Heger, accompanied by the town law and two armed deputies.

Longarm nodded and said, ''Link told Miss Iona and me about that as he lay dying this evening. That was the rub as far as stealing all that money before Heger could pass it on was concerned. Ritter was for killing you as well, sir. But that left those two deputies who'd have to be killed as well, and the two cooler heads talked Ritter out of a total bloodbath that might have led to Sattler's door in any case. Once the money was missing, the rest of you were bound to ask who'd had it last. But nobody but the actual donors and the few authorized to move the money from the bank so it could eventually get

178

to those so-called Ruggles sisters were supposed to *know* there'd been that much in Heger's vault."

Somebody wanted to know why he didn't think the Ruggles sisters were the Ruggles sisters.

Longarm said, "I know they ain't. But forget 'em. Their only crime was making noise. They never even managed to take money under false pretenses. They never knew about the collection for a drought this way. The three sneaks never let them hear your offer. Sattler was the one that needed a good alibi. They agreed that had they just killed Heger and taken the money, Sattler would be the most logical suspect. So they needed some razzle-dazzle to make us look under a heap of other shells for the pea."

He took another drag to compose his thoughts, knowing some of them were already finding his tale hard to follow, and continued. "Ritter was sort of proud of his recorded killings. So he'd kept a bunch of old reward posters on himself and rival killers. He'd long since rid himself of the incriminating LeMat revolver he'd used often enough to have it noted by the law. But it was easy enough to pick up another at a hock-shop over to the county seat. I could prove that by a wire from your county sheriff if there was any need to. Seeing there ain't, just picture the town law he trusted and an Irish cowhand he'd done business with showing up late that same night, along with the foreman of this Lazy B. Heger had quarters above his shop. His one and only assistant, Helga Pilger, was asleep out back over the carriage house. They forced Heger to open his vault and hand over all that money. Then the four of 'em went out to the carriage shed and hitched up Heger's shay. When the sleepy gal called down, it was Ritter, not her boss, who allowed he was going somewhere the sleepy-eyed gal had no call to remember all that accurately. When you ask a sleepy question in High Dutch and somebody mutters back at you in High Dutch, you just go back to bed."

He took another drag, grimaced, and said, "The heroic outlaws took the poor gunsmith far enough out on the prairie for privacy, filled him full of lead, and here's where they got tricky. Sattler tore back to his office in the town hall to look innocent, being the most likely of the three to look guilty. Link drove the shay over to the county seat under cover of darkness, trailing his cow pony behind it, so's he could abandon it there and send a Western Union night letter, composed by Wolf Ritter, saying the undersigned, Heger, had spotted such a notorious crook and could use the reward. They sent it to my more distant office to give themselves some working time. Meanwhile, Ritter, who enjoyed that sort of work the most, pony-packed the body back to the shop, locked it in the vault to sort of marinate, and dragged more red herrings across their trail. He left those wanted papers where they'd be found. I did find them, and came to the wrong conclusion. He left the LeMat he'd just used on Heger in Heger's front window, priced so high nobody would buy it before a sucker such as this child noticed it. When I did, I jumped to some of the conclusions they wanted me to. Taking the telegram from Heger and all those wanted flyers in his work shop at face value, I figured the man I couldn't find to talk to had spotted a known killer and been killed by the same or run off with all that money after I found out about the money. When I *did* suspect Werner Sattler of anything, late in the game, I was still mixed up. I was so busy wondering why a lawman would cover up for an outlaw with a handsome bounty on him that I never had time to ask about that money before he more or less confessed he'd done *something* wrong by bolting from that earlier hearing. But he did, and so let's forget him and his pals for a minute.''

The deputy coroner demanded, ''How do those other outlaws, seven in all, tie into the murder of Horst Heger?''

Longarm said, ''They don't directly. As I told you at that earlier hearing after the shootout in the saloon, Breen, Dawson, Fawcett, and Walters came to town to rob your bank of other money entirely. They had no call to rob a missing gunsmith they'd never laid eyes on. The four of them hid out with that trash washwoman, the late Brunhilda Maler. Which one of them recalled her from her earlier days as a soiled dove ain't important. They might or might not have cracked the bank vault in Sappa Crossing, like they did the ones in other Kansas towns of late. But then somebody neither sets of crooks had anything to do with sent me crashing through the window of Heger's shop and inspired Werner Sattler and his boys, acting in good faith against total strangers, to arrest Fingers Fawcett and Juicy Joe as suspicious characters.''

''Then who pegged that shot at you?'' someone naturally asked.

Longarm said, ''Nobody important to this case. Think of it as a mean kid prank. What's important is that the confusion worked to the advantage of Ritter and his pals. Tiny Tim Breen and Slick Dawson, rattled by the unexpected arrests of *their* pals, hung around town long enough for me to get into a saloon shootout with 'em. Then a pair of *worse* crooks backed my play, partly to avoid having to look yellow in front of men who knew them and partly because Ritter, as Trooper O'Donnel for Gawd's sake, *liked* to kill total strangers. So I was really taken for a buggy ride by what had started out as simple slickery. I might or might not have fallen for the first simple plans to have a federal lawman declare the notorious Wolf Ritter and not a small-town marshal had ridden off with all that money, but once other events conspired to confound me further . . .''

Kurt Morgenstern asked insistently, ''*Aber weiso* would the real Wolfgang von Ritterhoff want anyone to think he'd ever been anywhere near Sappa Crossing already?''

Longarm explained. ''So we'd think he'd gone somewheres else after committing another crime with his famous LeMat, of course. My boss, Marshal Billy Vail, thought a High Dutch-speaking community would be a swell place for High Dutch crooks to hide out in, as soon as he'd had occasion to think about such a place. But Ritter had established himself in these parts as an Irish top hand, and he figured he'd look even less like his real self if we figured he'd pulled another of his crimes just passing through. Let me get back to the way I was thrown off his scent by other skunks.''

He flicked ash from the tip of his cheroot and continued. ''With the safecrackers she'd known and cherished dead or locked up, old Brunhilda was stuck with plenty of nitroglycerine and confided that to another occasional caller, who worked as a part-time town deputy when he wasn't pussyfooting around by the river the way randy young gents are tempted to when they don't have much money and an old bat don't charge much. He knew we were searching for a missing gunsmith and a heap of money because he got to hang about the town hall more than most crooks. So he told a pal, and they put two and two together to figure wrong about what was really in Heger's vault. You all know how *that* turned out. Most of you were at that other hearing earlier when I finally started to notice how many leads seemed to end where a town marshal vouched unsupported. As I'd been about to say when he bolted, I was having a time figuring out how some parts fit together. I found it tough to buy a wanted outlaw on the run with a gun to be sold on *consignment*. Yet old Werner kept assuring me all my handy suspects were known to him as a bunch of local boys. I had a little trouble deciding how even a famous outlaw would have known about that secret fund for the Ruggles sisters unless someone in town told him about it. I couldn't see Horst Heger confiding he had a fortune in his vault to a man he'd just recognized as a holdup man. But you all saw how Sattler bolted, and now he's in the smokehouse with a bullet in his chest and his head busted in with a rolling pin, so are there any more questions?''

The deputy coroner declared that since earlier witnesses had described the wild fight inside this very house, along with what all three crooks had admitted in plain English, he aimed to dismiss this last witness with a commendation for a job well done.

It still took them until almost midnight to break up and get on back to town with the three bodies. So Longarm was yawning as he groped his way out to the stable and started to saddle the bay while telling it they'd have to go easy on its lamed paint pal.

Iona MacSorley joined him there in the warm horsy darkness in what seemed her nightgown. He hoped for her sake she was wearing boots. He howdied her, and explained he meant to get the livery mounts home before the sun rose high enough to sweat them. She murmured, "*Athair* is fast asleep in his own wing of the house, and nobody comes near my quarters before breakfast time if they know what's good for them!"

He said, "That's swell. We've all had a rough day and you'll feel better after a good night's sleep, Miss Iona."

She asked, "Why didn't you tell them it was I who took that shot at you in front of the gunsmith's window? Just to get you to come back here for the night, of course. I'd have hit you had I been aiming at you."

He nodded soberly and said, "I saw you nail that yard dog with a hip shot, Miss Iona. I had no call to cause you embarrassment or mix your neighbors up with more details than they needed to get down. So let's agree no harm was done and say no more about it."

She stepped closer. He saw she really was standing there in a thin nightgown as she purred, "Now that we've settled that, let me make it up to you, Custis. Come back to my quarters with me or, for that matter, would you like to climb up in the hayloft with me here and now?"

He ignored the hand she'd placed on his sleeve to shake his head and reply, firmly but not unkindly, "I aim to make it to Cedar Bend around sunrise, Miss Iona. So why don't you run on to bed and I'll just be on my way."

He knew she was wearing boots when she stamped a foot wetly on the stable floor and demanded, "What's wrong? Why do you slight me so? Don't you think I'm pretty? Have I done something to offend you?"

Longarm smiled wryly down at her in the dim light and said, "Nobody could be as pretty as you think you are, but you ain't bad looking, Miss Iona. As for how offensive I find you, I ain't got time to list 'em all. Let's just say I don't cotton to gals who shoot dogs just for acting like dogs, snap at the hired help just because they ain't allowed to snap back, and peg shots at me just because I never swooned at the sight of so much loveliness.''

She sobbed, ''I told you I was only teasing, darling!''

But he said, ''I ain't your darling. I don't *like* you, Miss Iona. I reckon what you done to that dog was what really disgusted me. I ain't so fussy. In my time I've swapped spit with gals I might not want to be seen in public with. I've gone farther than that with gals I reckon some lawmen would have arrested. But I've never been the darling of anyone as spoiled rotten and mean-natured as you. So I'll be on my way now, and you'd best stand aside if you don't want me leading these two ponies across that silk nightgown with stable muck on all eight hooves.''

So she got out of the way, saying dreadful things about his mother and his manhood as he mounted out in the moonlight, ticked the brim of his Stetson to her, and rode off at a trot before she could run in the house and get a gun.

Longarm laughed as he reined in on a distant rise to get his bearings as he lit a smoke. Then he told his mount, ''That wagon trace to Cedar Bend is yonder, beyond that clump of soap weed. I know you both think me a fool. Some night, when I'm all alone in some strange hotel with a copy of the *Police Gazette* and a hard-on, I'm likely to cuss myself for passing up anything that perky and sweet-smelling. But I really didn't like her and, even if I had, good old Osage Olive will be waiting for us over in Cedar Bend come morning, just in time for breakfast too.''

He carefully doubled the match stem so he wouldn't set the dry prairie ablaze, and wryly added, ''All right, Osage Olive ain't half as pretty, but it wouldn't be possible for such a selfish little snot like Iona to move her hips so generously. So Powder River and let her buck!''

Watch for

LONGARM AND BIG TROUBLE IN BODIE

201st in the bold LONGARM series
from Jove

Coming in September!

A special offer for people who enjoy reading the best Westerns published today.

WESTERNS!

NO OBLIGATION

Mail the coupon below

To start your subscription and receive 2 FREE WESTERNS, fill out the coupon below and mail it today. We'll send your first shipment which includes 2 FREE BOOKS as soon as we receive it.